Thomas C. Hinkle rode and hunted the Kansas plains when covered wagons still carried men westward. One of his most exciting boyhood memories was seeing the horse, *Comanche*, only surviver of General Custer's last battle. Besides writing 23 books, Hinkle was also a physician and minister.

# BLACK
# STORM

## BY THOMAS C. HINKLE

**SBS** SCHOLASTIC BOOK SERVICES
New York Toronto London Auckland Sydney

To the Memory of

**BLACK STORM**

Copyright 1929 by William Morrow and Co., Inc. Copyright renewed by Rolland Theodore Hinkle and Thomas Clark Hinkle, Jr. This edition is published by Scholastic Book Services, a division of Scholastic Magazines, Inc. by arrangement with William Morrow and Company, Inc.

10th printing.................................March 1971

Printed in the U.S.A.

# AUTHOR'S NOTE

BLACK STORM was a real character.

The late John Campbell, one of the most skilled horsemen of the old West, often told me the story of Black Storm when I was a youth, herding cattle in the hills near Fort Riley and Junction City, Kansas.

Joe Bain, under a different name, was also a real character—more of this splendid youth later.

It will be seen that a great part of Black Storm's story is in Kansas, and it will be seen also that he traveled, after getting free from the men who stole him, far into the West. It was known by many old horsemen that he was seen at one time as far as Montana, but I have shortened his history, from several years, to the space of little more than one and a half. Black Storm was never successfully ridden until that dramatic day when Joe Bain mounted him with fully fifty men gathered about the horse corral to watch the event. Black Storm pitched for a full half hour as I have related, for when it was seen that Joe Bain might stay on, the event was timed. That scene is set down as it actually happened and was told to me by Mr. Campbell, who saw it all.

The complete change of mind of Black Storm toward Joe Bain after that dramatic incident can be explained, I think, in only one way. I do not think it was merely because he felt he was conquered, for he threw many men after this—threw them with all his old lightning-like quickness, when they mounted him, as he had of old.

No, Black Storm gave in to Joe Bain with all his heart because he *wanted* love and kindness—he was starving for it. And for the first time in his life that day, he found a man who would not hurt him. There is no doubt but that exhaustion itself, in that hour, at last brought the horse to the full realization that Joe had not hurt him, and once this was realized, he longed with all his soul to love the youth who dismounted, holding his old red handkerchief to his own nose to stop the flow of blood.

My love for Joe Bain has made it hard for me to keep him in the background in Black Storm's story. I asked Mr. Campbell, who was one of the men who timed the pitching of Black Storm—that day with Joe Bain—how it was that Joe remained on the horse. Mr. Campbell said, "We never saw anything like it, but as near as we could tell the youth *kept time with the pitching.*"

At the time he was, for his age, one of the most skillful, resourceful and trusted cattle foremen the old West ever knew.

I have taken only one real liberty in the story—that was the actual place where Black

Storm battled with Joe Bain. It was near a town in Montana in the days when the Texas Longhorns were being driven into the Far West from Abilene, Kansas. Every incident in this story is based on a fact. Some of them I have seen myself while living with horses and dogs on the plains. For instance, I saw a horse roped, and saw him meet death by rearing and falling backward in the tragic incident I describe of the wild stallion.

The incident also is true of Black Storm being able somehow to sense the treacherous quicksand in the river. Many horses of that day learned this and one summer, while herding cattle near the sandy Republican River near Junction City, Kansas, I rode a horse on the river bed that would never step in quicksand if allowed to pick his way.

Mr. Campbell told me of many incidents in the life of Black Storm as he knew them and said that more than once some irate man, who had bought the horse only to learn he could not be tamed, wanted to kill him, but always his sheer beauty saved him.

It was known that he survived not only the savage winter in the wild, as I have described, but others also, and there *were scars on his hind legs, near the hamstrings, scars that those who saw them said could have been made by nothing but gray wolves;* so it is most certain he battled and won in his battling with these beasts.

Mr. Campbell, inured to the feats of horses as he and others were, marveled at the *endurance* of Black Storm in his amazing races across the plains, when he ran down two and even three sets of horses while men were trying to rope him—it would have been unbelievable unless one had seen it with his own eyes.

The incidents at the cow town of Wichita were real, and so likewise was the prairie fire in which two men lost their lives.

I have been caught on a horse in one or two of the fearful dust storms that now and then sweep over western Kansas, and I also know what it is to be on a horse and caught in a hail storm. My description of what Black Storm did in these storms is what I have seen a horse do.

The tragedy that came to Black Storm by getting a piece of flint in his foot is also based on a fact—and I have not half described the pitiful condition to which I have seen a horse reduced by such an accident.

Some years ago I made a trip West to see an old cow man who, in his day, was a great rider and who drove one of the first herds of Texas Longhorns from Abilene, Kansas, to Wyoming. It was my extreme good fortune that, as a boy, I worked for this man, herding cattle. I had seen many horses pitch, of course—but it had never occurred to me to think of the *length of time* even the strongest horse would pitch. This man was no moving-picture cowboy—he was one of the real ones of the old West. I knew he would know about this if any man would and I asked him the length of time the strongest outlaw pitched hard and incessantly with a rider.

He said, "About ten minutes—now and then fifteen minutes, but not often, and mighty few ever went twenty minutes—but Black Storm!" the old cowman mused, his eyes suddenly lighting with a far-away look—"he was a wonderful horse—we all knew him; yes, he pitched that day for the full half hour—that was a wonderful horse and a wonderful boy that rode him —we always called Joe a boy—always something so nice and quiet and kind about him. I remember that when he wanted one of the men to carry out some order, Joe would tell him so easy, always smiling. When he gave his order like that, he never had any trouble with the boys, and, young as he was, none of the older men ever had envy toward him, but were only too glad to have him for a boss." The old man paused for a moment, his eyes narrowed, looking far into the hills beyond to the West and for a moment seemed to forget my presence; then dropping his elbows on his knees, his head in his hands as if better to shut out all that interfered with the memory of his days in the old West, he said slowly, reminiscently, "I've known many men and many horses in my day, yet never but one Joe Bain, and never but one Black Storm."

T. C. H.

🐎🐎🐎 🐎🐎🐎 *Contents* 🐎🐎🐎 🐎🐎🐎

*A wild, black streak shot through the air!*

## Chapter I

## BLACK STORM

*N*EAR a frontier cattle town of old Kansas on that memorable morning, John McDonald, the cattle owner of the Chisholm Range, stood in the center of a corral holding the reins of a beautiful horse—a coal-black gelding. Fully forty cowboys sat on the corral fence looking. The great black horse stood with his head high, a wild light of fear in his eyes and he quivered in every muscle as he looked back at the stockily built man standing by the saddle.

"Well, here he is," said McDonald to his men. "They call him Black Storm. I got him cheap because nobody can ride him. He's been tried all the way from Texas to Kansas. No trouble to saddle him. He'll stand perfect as you see," and the boss moved away, leaving the horse standing. "There he is; he belongs to the man who can ride him!"

Instant excitement prevailed.

Certainly here was a good horse! Jet-black, long-limbed, graceful flowing mane and tail. But the men hesitated. Here was no broncho. A broncho may pitch violently but he is small —small and therefore has not the strength of a big horse, and the broncho could not do to a rider what a big horse could—especially a horse like this! Muscles of power were there. These men knew it. They had reason to know. They were not tenderfeet. They were among the best riders in the old American West, which meant they were the best riders in the world.

Black Storm was not hard to approach. He was easy to approach. That was his way.

The first man vaulted into the saddle.

A wild, black streak shot through the air; once, twice, thrice—the man fell hard.

Another mounted. The same thing. Then another and another and another. Twenty men Black Storm threw, and threw them like lightning.

Laughing and spitting dust from their mouths and some of them a little blood, they set up a wild shout. "Where's Joe Bain, Mac? Here's one he can't stick. Get him in!"

A half mile away they found him.

Joe Bain, the silent, came riding in—Joe Bain, but a twenty-one-year-old youth—yet the able, trusted foreman over all the McDonald men and the tens of thousands of Texas Longhorns.

The men sat as thick as crows on the top poles of the corral while shouting to Joe Bain, "You can have him, Joe, if you want him! He's a purty hoss! But pick a nice soft place to light in! We all wanted a haystack but couldn't find any!"

The tall, black horse stood in the center of the corral, his eyes shining, his ears, not standing stiff, but moving back and forth. Joe Bain noted this as he walked slowly forward. On came the man; the horse shied a little, then stood trembling while Joe slowly came up. He looked at the horse's head. He was wide between the ears. He looked into his eyes. They were not devil eyes, they were eyes of a mighty good horse but a terribly frightened one. Joe looked at the horse's sides. They were bleeding from the spurs of the men. Joe stood looking in silence, then bent down, removed his spurs and tossed them aside; and he threw his quirt after them.

"Open the gate, Jim," Joe ordered the nearest man. "I'll mount him outside."

Outside on the wild, level prairie, Joe carefully examined the cinch of the saddle, while the horse stood in a tremble, his eyes set back on his man.

Quietly, slowly, Bain gathered the reins, and then like a cat he was in the saddle.

Wild yells from many cowboys rent the air. The great black flashed up and down, whirled and leaped, reared high and leaped and whirled again, then up—and then that terrible drop to the earth on four stiff legs; and again he leaped with a greyhound leap, stopped short, leaped again. More wild tricks he knew than any pitching horse ever seen on a range of the West. Up and down with terrific plunges, and up and down again, and still the long, lithe form of a sun-tanned youth held. It seemed impossible that any man could stand all this and stay, but he did, and stayed on far beyond the limit of most pitching horses. A full half hour he stayed! And then, with a hush among the men, the tall, slim youth, blood running from his nose, dismounted from a groaning, foam-covered, quivering horse. The youth held his red bandanna handkerchief a minute to his bleeding nose, while patting the horse gently on the neck. He moved around in front of him, took the horse's nose gently in his hands, and the horse held down to him, closed his eyes and breathed peacefully.

Then the miracle. With low, soothing words Joe Bain put his foot in the stirrup, mounted slowly, and as slowly rode the horse a quarter of a mile on the prairie, rode back, dismounted and again held the horse's head in his hands, petted him and talked to him gently.

"Thank you, Mac," said Bain simply to McDonald. "He's a good horse. Somebody gave him a bad start, that's all."

Bain fingered in his pocket for a trinket he had long carried. It was a bright silver star with a pin at the back. While the horse stood with his head down, Joe fixed the star permanently in the head-band of the bridle.

For a long time all the cowmen stood about talking of the horse, looking at him, admiring him. Then Joe Bain mounted again and with Black Storm fully at ease Joe said, "Well, boys, it's time we were going on with the cattle." All hands were soon ready and in a brief time the long herd of Longhorns, temporarily halted here for rest, were started toward the east.

For two weeks it had not rained and as the vast herds, with Joe Bain on the black horse at their head, moved slowly forward into the deeper-cut cattle trails, a great cloud of dust floated up to settle down over cattle and men. At times through the dusty veil something in the morning sunlight flashed and gleamed and glistened. It was the silver star that Joe had fixed on the head-band of Black Storm's bridle.

Two of the cowboys were riding on either

side of Joe and admiring Black Storm. They were nearing the river and at this moment John McDonald came galloping up. It was always necessary to swim the Longhorns across the river here as there was no bridge except a pontoon and this was too frail to support these vast herds of cattle. It had always been Joe Bain who had ridden at the head of the herd on a trusted horse—one that would walk quietly into the deepest stream and swim, thus leading the cattle who would follow the familiar figure of Joe.

But now Joe was on the erstwhile intractable Black Storm. McDonald did not believe that the black horse could be trusted to enter the river and swim across in front of the herd. He was afraid also that if the horse did enter the stream he might, when below his depth, become frightened and so endanger the fearless rider.

McDonald rode up and said, "Joe, you have a wonderful horse—but maybe you had better not try to lead the cattle across this time—I don't like to let one of the other boys try it either—but if you will take another horse—"

"You wait and see us, Mac!" said Joe. "Black Storm may hesitate a little at the edge of the water but when he knows what I want he'll go right in. I'll go ahead a little and talk to him."

And still without spur or quirt Joe cantered on to the margin of the deep stream not far forward. He rode down the sloping bank to the water's edge where Black Storm stopped of his own accord. Joe dismounted and took the horse's nose in his hands and petted him saying, "We'll swim on across the river, Stormy, we'll go right across." Bain knew the horse did not understand the words but he knew he understood the spirit behind them. Joe mounted. Black Storm turned a little away from the the stream but Joe pressed the rein on his neck, at the same time gently urging him to go in. Black Storm stood for an instant, his trim fore hoofs at the edge of the water, his ears moving nervously back and forth as he looked across the river.

"Come, Stormy!" said Joe, leaning over and patting him on the neck—"straight in and right across!"

Black Storm stepped nervously with his front feet a little, but he did not back away an inch, then he held his head down and looked at the water. He put one foot out and pawed the water a little, then looked down, then up and across.

"Come, Stormy!" Joe repeated, still patting him, and with that Black Storm surged in, his great black body sinking until only his head and upper neck were out of the water, and he was swimming like a veteran.

"Did you ever see anything like it?" exclaimed McDonald to three of his men who sat their horses beside him watching Joe and his horse.

"Joe's got that horse won for certain," said the little under-foreman, Charlie Bliss.

"It's Joe's way," said McDonald, "and that horse has won Joe as completely as Joe has won him—look at him swim! Acts like it was all perfectly natural for him—a smart horse that—you wait and see! In a month Joe will have him performing all kinds of tricks."

The Longhorn cattle had promptly entered the stream and were swimming behind Black Storm. They filled the river with a great mass of tremendous horns—some of them six and seven feet from tip to tip. As they swam their long horns frequently struck one another with a dull, clacking sound. But Black Storm did not seem at all concerned by the mass of swimming cattle behind him. He swam rapidly, his ears cocked forward, his large eyes looking eagerly across the river. For the first time a man sat on his back talking gently to him and now and then lovingly patting that part of his neck above the water—a man who seemed so quiet and kind and who did not hurt.

Black Storm reached the opposite side, plunged up the sloping bank, alert and ready for Joe's slightest command. Arriving upon the level valley above the river, Joe waved to McDonald and Charlie Bliss, and then started on ahead of the cattle, now moving up the valley toward the bluffs on the east. McDonald, Charlie Bliss and the other cowboys were now swimming the stream behind the cattle and presently the whole herd was across. From their position behind the cattle they could see at the head of the long herd the form of a beautiful black horse moving in the distance.

Charlie Bliss laughed nervously. "Mac, I'm still looking at that horse, wondering if he'll take a sudden turn with Joe and start pitching again!"

McDonald did not reply, and he too was still a little in doubt as he kept his eyes almost constantly on the distant Black Storm.

At last the advance of the herd reached the bluffs where the trail led up the hillside toward the highlands beyond. Several cowboys with John McDonald galloped up to Joe who was still riding at the head of the advancing cattle, and together they turned them up the hill trail.

The Longhorns moved in long, narrow lines —cattle of many colors, red, dun, black, brindle, fawn and some of them red and black, and white and black spotted. When the men riding ahead of the herd reached the summit of the hill range, they were so intent in their work of turning the cattle in the right direction, that they did not look any distance on either side of them, and, once the cattle were headed east, these foremost riders continued to follow near the front as before.

On the high summit of the hill, Joe, who was riding near John McDonald, turned and said, "Mac, I'm going to turn off here and show Helen my new horse."

"She'll go into raptures over him," McDonald smiled, and Joe galloped away toward the ranch buildings that showed as tiny dots on the plain toward the north.

Joe had not gone a mile when he saw another rider coming rapidly from the north to meet him. It was Helen McDonald, the daughter of John. In the distance Helen had seen the herd of cattle as it came up on the highlands and now she recognized Joe Bain and, even at a distance, the magnificence of the black horse on which he was mounted.

They came together and brought their horses to a stand.

"Hello, Joe!" she greeted him with enthusiasm. "So glad to see you—seemed as if you'd never come"—and then Helen burst out, "Oh! Joe, where *did* you get that beautiful horse?"

Briefly, Joe told her while she dismounted and came up to Black Storm. She reached out her hand and he held his nose toward her in a wondering manner, while she touched him gently and patted his head.

"Why, Joe!" she exclaimed, a frown of indignation on her face, "just look at his poor sides where men have been spurring him!"

"I know it," said Joe. "He's had awful cruel treatment," and both of them looked at the wounds still fresh on Black Storm's sides where the spurs had cut through his beautiful coat.

"That's the notion all over the West," said Joe. "The men seem to think that to ride a horse they have to spur him, but I never did believe it. Black Storm has been made wild and crazed by it. They've hurt him so much, he has been afraid of everybody. I could see it as I watched and studied him before I mounted him this morning. He was called an outlaw of the worst sort because they could not conquer him."

"Of course," said Helen, stroking and patting his neck. "He's not like the other horses, I can see that. He's got pride and spirit and would never give in. I like him because he is that way— Oh! *isn't* he a beauty!" Then she broke off suddenly. "Joe, he looks as if he could run like the wind. Will you race me—my new sorrel is fast, you know!"

"Sure, I will!" said Joe, smiling, "and I'll give you a good start."

Helen leaped into her saddle. "How far shall we run, Joe?" she asked excitedly.

"To that lone cedar in the north—that's about a half mile!"

Joe sat quietly in the saddle, while Helen

started her nervous sorrel out ahead, holding him with difficulty. When she was about fifty yards distant, she called back, "This far enough?"

"Go on that much further!" shouted Joe.

"You'll never catch me!" Helen shouted back, and she let the big sorrel out a little faster, looking back toward Joe for the signal. When out fully a hundred yards, Joe waved his hand to go; Helen touched her sorrel with the quirt. He leaped like a shot across the level plain as Helen bent low over him. Chestnut, her sorrel, was good—she knew that. She lay low on his neck as he flew along—a quarter of a mile. The next time Joe would want an even start. Then she heard the thunder of hoofbeats behind her and in an instant a great, black horse shot past and still on like a puff of smoke from a rifle—and came up to the cedar a full hundred yards ahead.

At the cedar tree, Helen dismounted. Joe was already on the ground, standing by Black Storm's side.

Without a word Helen came up to Black Storm who was breathing heavily but with his eyes alert. She took his head in her hands and he was not afraid.

"Oh, Joe!" she said, "he's wonderful—just *wonderful!* Why, Chestnut has outrun every- thing on the range. Oh! you beauty!" she ex claimed, patting the horse's head. Then she suddenly turned and said with anxiety in her voice, "I hope none of the horse thieves will steal him," and she looked with deep concern at Joe.

"I've been thinking of that, Helen," Joe said, "and I'm going to use extra care. At night, I will tie him in the shed near the house and keep him under padlock."

At this moment as Helen walked around Black Storm to get a better look at him, she chanced to glance down on the valley.

"Oh! look, Joe!" she exclaimed, "more and more cattle!"

"Yes," said Joe, "there will be ten thousand head on the valley when we get them all in and all new and strange—strange and nervous and always ready to give us trouble."

"Plenty of chances for a bad stampede," said Helen with a serious look on her face. "But you've got Black Storm," she added brightening. "I believe he could turn them."

"I believe he could," said Joe, "but I hope we won't have to try him. There'd be great danger in a stampede here with rivers on the two sides of us. We've decided to watch these new cattle day and night for a time. We're going to use the boys in day and night shifts. It's going to be mighty bad especially if heavy rains come and send the rivers to the flood."

## Chapter II
## THE RACE

**D**URING the next four weeks Black Storm became known to every man on the range for miles around; everyone in the cattle town also knew him and all eyes were centered on him when Joe Bain rode his beautiful, proud-stepping horse into the main street.

As soon as Black Storm had found a man he could trust he turned about from the wild outlaw he had been to the most tractable and teachable of horses, and withal, one of the most lovable. Joe's love for his horse made him extremely patient with him, and as soon as Black Storm knew what Joe wanted he did it instantly.

So in these weeks of training the two were drawn closer and closer together. Joe taught Black Storm to kneel, to lie down with his head up and then to lie down at full length, his eyes closed, as if he were sound asleep. The horse was also taught to come up and lay his head on Joe's shoulder. And many times while Joe was asking him to perform for interested onlookers, Black Storm would come up without any command and lay his head on Joe's shoulder. At first, when he did this without the command, Joe thought that he had misunderstood but when after the days had gone by and the horse did this time after time, it was seen by Joe and his friends that Black Storm did this to show his affection for his master. And after he had done this he would often put his nose on Joe's cheek, while uttering low sounds that told as plainly as he could, that he was happy with Joe Bain.

Finally, Joe taught Black Storm to sit down, and this trick in particular was the delight of the boys in the town where Joe had several times had his horse perform for them. Indeed, so popular did the horse become with the boys and men, that when the townspeople held their first summer festival at the new fair grounds, the women got Helen McDonald to talk to Joe about it, and the result was that Joe agreed to ride Black Storm in for the entertainment of

the spectators. Joe was also induced to enter
Black Storm in the race.

The day came with soft warm sunshine, the
green grass and many colored wild flowers over
all the place. By nine o'clock many of the flower
blooms had been plucked by women and
children, for from far and near the people began to gather as the fairgrounds opened.

At last a large group of boys and men
gathered near the gate and began impatiently
to wait. A number of pretty horses were ridden
in by the men but the boys took little notice of
them. Finally a boy shouted, "There he comes!
Black Storm and Joe Bain—and Helen McDonald! Look at Black Storm! Here he comes!"
And a great shout went up while the boys and
men began pushing and surging toward the
gate. And then the throng separated, making a
long line as Joe Bain rode in, smiling at the
eagerness of the boys. And Helen McDonald
smiled also although she knew that the crowd
scarcely noticed her chestnut sorrel—for all eyes
were centered on the proud, high-stepping, majestic Black Storm. He came in with his beautiful head held high, his ears moving back and
forth nervously, his great flowing mane and tail
perfectly groomed; around his breast and
shoulders a white leather martingale; on his
head a white leather bridle, a bow of blue rib-
bon on the head-band that Helen had tied there

with loving hands. A shining silver star was set in each of the four corners of the black saddle blanket with its striking white border; and sitting on the horse, a large Western sombrero on his head, buckskin chaps with leather fringes, a soft shirt, open at the collar, riding without spur or quirt, sat the famous youthful Joe Bain, one of the greatest riders the old West ever knew.

A little beyond the long lines of men and boys stood a large group of women, and while they looked at the beautiful black gelding there came in a chorus many "oh's!" and "ah's!" as they admired him.

As Joe rode among the watchers, some of the smaller boys crowded so close to Black Storm that the smile on Joe's face changed to a look of anxiety. The boys behind had pushed in so close that for the moment those nearest were helpless to move back. With a word Joe ordered Black Storm to halt. The horse's ears turned with quick nervous movements, showing that the situation was a strain on him, but he did not move an inch while Joe sat on his back and told the crowd to give way. When the path was clear Joe rode forward to the enclosure which had been arranged for him. Already at that point a man stood shouting to the people to gather there and witness the performing of the famous Black Storm.

From far and near the crowd came. They mounted the low broad seats, in a wide circle about the place, while others stood in the rear watching.

Joe first rode Black Storm once around the circle so that all might see him, then in the center he dismounted and removed both saddle and bridle, the while speaking low to Black Storm and petting him often with his hands. Joe spoke so low that the people barely heard him, but they could tell what he said by what the horse did. First, Black Storm knelt, then slowly lay down and stretched himself on the ground, his eyes closed. He then got up and, at another word from Joe, stood on his hind feet, and hard though this was for him, he moved about by awkward, jerky movements for a little and did not drop on all four feet again until Joe told him. Once more Joe spoke to him, then stepped out to the edge of the circle. The horse walked out near the people and paced slowly around the circle, coming to a stop when he stood before Joe. Joe patted his head and again spoke to him. Black Storm walked to the center of the circle and did the last thing Joe asked of him. He sat down like a dog. The boys shouted their delight, but although the horse only moved his ears back and forth showing his wonder at it all, this merely made the boys shout the more. Black Storm now looked steadily toward Joe for the order. Joe called out to him, "That's all now except roll over, Stormy!" Black Storm lay down and rolled clear over— twice, first on one side and then on the other, then got up and shook himself vigorously and stood still, looking at Joe and waiting.

As Joe moved over and put the saddle and bridle on him the crowd cheered and began moving toward the race track. Great excitement was now on because Black Storm was to run in a race with seven other horses. These horses were already on the track with their riders and the bell at this moment sounded for all who were to enter the race to appear at once and make ready. It was to be a race where every rider must be a man. Joe Bain had insisted on this since he knew it would be necessary for him to ride Black Storm, and it would give all the horses a more equal chance, although it was noticed that some of the other horses were ridden by rather small men. The horses already on the track were known for their unusual speed.

The race which had been carefully arranged for the fairgrounds had an unusual significance. It was to be, in fact, an elimination contest, the winning horse being the one that would run three days later with a famous racing mare owned by one of the officers at Fort Riley. A race between her and the best of the field here

had been arranged for the maneuvers of the
Seventh Cavalry on the Republican River
valley—a gala event which the people from the
town loved to behold. This race with the mare,
a beautiful sorrel with four white stocking legs,
was set to start on the valley at two o'clock of
the appointed day.

There was therefore unusual interest in the
race about to start for it was known that almost
to a certainty there would be no tie. What horse
then would be the one to enter the contest with
the famous mare of the Seventh Cavalry? That
was the question that was asked and talked
about excitedly as the horses with their riders
leaped out on the track and began rearing and
plunging in their nervousness to be off.

The moment that Joe rode out on the track
among the seven long-legged, leaping, plunging horses, all knew the event was about to
happen. Black Storm suddenly became extremely nervous. It seemed that he understood
exactly and that he did not want any of them
to get the start of him. Time after time as he
and the others approached the judges' stand he
was so far ahead, in spite of Joe's efforts, that
they had to go back for a new start. At last Joe
saw there never would be a fair start unless he
gave a great advantage to the entire field and
although he disliked extremely to do this still
it was not in Joe Bain to take unfair advantage

of any man. He rode close to the judges' stand and said, "I won't halt things any longer. I'll ride back and start, and when you see me coming let the field go!"

This was an unusual thing and every man that heard it knew it would come only from Joe Bain.

"All right, Joe," one of the judges called out. "It seems to be the only way."

Joe cantered Black Storm back and still back and back. The crowd thought he would never turn, but at last he did. At the same time the other horses were moving in excellent formation down to the wire. Then the crowd saw Joe Bain coming, and when he was still fully fifty yards from the wire the gong sounded "Go!" for all the other horses were just at the line. They shot away and the race was on with Black Storm a full fifty yards behind, on a mile track.

Down the course the horses raced, a cloud of dust enveloping them completely. And then Black Storm swept into the dust cloud and the throng of people stood to their feet to look. They could see nothing but dust—and still dust at the half-mile post—and dust still at the three-quarter post—and then on the home stretch they saw pointing his nose out of the dust a great black horse. On he came, a length, two lengths, three and still on—his nostrils wide, his eyes ablaze, his hoofs thundering down the stretch like the fire of musketry. The crowd went wild as Black Storm thundered under the wire nearly as far ahead of the field as he was behind them when he started.

Helen McDonald's sorrel, ridden by Charlie Bliss, the under-foreman, had been second in the race, but Helen was overjoyed that Black Storm had won in such a remarkable handicap. She was the first to greet him as Joe dismounted, with his horse breathing hard in the midst of a throng of admirers. Some boys came crowding in. "We want to pet Black Storm," they said.

"Very well," said Joe. "He doesn't seem to be afraid of you boys." But Helen and some of the women who knew Black Storm's former history gasped when Joe picked up a boy and set him in the saddle, then another, and when three of them sat upon him, Black Storm turned his head around curiously, looked at their feet, and paid no more attention to them.

"He's looking to see if they have spurs on," said Joe, a slight frown crossing his face. "That's what he dreads above everything else —you see his sides still show the scars where riders have spurred him. Black Storm's all right if men won't hurt him, but he won't stand spurs or the quirt. He's mortally afraid of them; they have cut him fearfully with whips—see!" and a half dozen women with Helen stood among the children as Joe rubbed slowly down on the horse's sweaty shoulders. "I can still feel the knots and scars on him where riders have lashed him and brought the blood; that's what made him such a terror."

At this moment there came a jangling sound from the crowd and Black Storm began to tremble and crowd close to Joe. Two cowboys with the big sharp Mexican wheel spurs, and one with small bells on his spurs passed near.

"You see, he can't stand that," said Joe. "He even knows the sound of the things. It troubles him and I think I'll take him away now."

After Joe had walked his horse about for a time a number of women came up close to Black Storm, began petting him affectionately and talking about his beauty and speed.

One of them looked at Joe and said, "Mr. Bain, I know that fine horse at Fort Riley, she's truly wonderful. I've seen her run but Black Storm has our hearts—do you think he will win against her—we hope he will!"

Joe's eyes narrowed a little. He smiled in his characteristic manner and said, "Well, the Major has promised to ride his mare—that will make our weights about equal and if you ladies come out on the valley to see that race I don't think you'll be disappointed."

"We'll be there!" they chorused in quick enthusiasm, "we'll be there—never a doubt about that!"

## Chapter III

### WITH THE SEVENTH CAVALRY

*L*ONG before this, Black Storm's fame, reports of his power and beauty had reached the officers and their wives at Fort Riley, only a few miles distant. The officers of the Seventh, always lovers of fine horses, were full of enthusiasm for the testing of Black Storm's speed and endurance with the famous white-stocking mare—the pride of the Seventh.

But the General commanding was almost boyish in his eagerness to see this race, for he had seen Black Storm, had walked around him with the eye of the skilled horseman, stroked his fine legs and so looked at him with an ever-growing admiration. Riding in at the Post that evening he had said to the Major, who owned the famous mare: "Major, for once the mare will have to give all she's got. That black is positively the most beautiful thing in horse flesh I've ever seen. He's got everything and that young cow man who rides him—well, there is nothing about riding that he does not know."

Two days passed. On the third morning, the sun came up over the hills in the east to shine soft and warm on the beautiful valley of the Republican. During the first morning hours nothing was to be seen on the valley save the vast carpet of green and the wild flowers of white and blue and gold. And as if waiting, the green willows stood along the river, hushed, pensive, fringing the water far in the west to the Creek of Dixon's, and the Republican River there showed its face of silver as it moved slowly down in the morning sun.

The people from town in large numbers drove over and took their position on the high north bluffs where they might with ease look down and view it all. By two o'clock a vast throng covered the hillside. At this moment a

bugle sounded to the east and out from the
little woods near the fort the old Seventh Cavalry came, the General leading, with Joe Bain
on Black Storm riding close beside him. The
mounted cavalry band, all on white horses,
came slowly behind the two riders, playing a
thrilling military air. Behind the band came a
troop of jet-black horses; following these a
troop of shining bays; behind these a troop of
grays; and still coming on a troop of chestnut
sorrels, all strikingly alike. The officers and men
were in the old blue dress-uniforms and Joe
Bain with his cowboy apparel was a striking
contrast to the others. Far above on the hillside
the ladies cheered with enthusiasm as Black
Storm, dressed as he was on the day of the race,
stepped majestically past, his eyes ablaze with
life and curiosity. He had been a little frightened when the cavalry band started playing,
but at an encouraging word from Joe he at once
accepted it as something he need have no fear
of.

The General, although himself on a fine Ken-
tucky horse he was proud of, could not take his
eyes from Black Storm, and when the long line
of people applauded he knew well that the ap-
plause was but for one creature—Black Storm.

The General turned and spoke a command
to the bugler riding just behind. The youth
blew a blast, giving the order, and the most

beautiful and romantic thing in the army began—a drill of the Seventh Cavalry on a carpet
of green on a Kansas valley—a drill of beautiful,
trained horses, all moving as one, now in a long
line, now in threes, now twos, now in whole
troops, all trotting or galloping forward. And
finally, just before the race was to begin, the
entire cavalry formed a hollow square, the
mounted band, on the white horses, in th:
center playing the spirited air of the popula:
song at that time, "Garry Owen."

When the band ceased playing, the General,
sitting his horse beside Joe Bain, gave the command, and twenty of the best buglers in the
United States army, including the chief bugler,
sounded call after call, playing in chords of har-
mony; and the older men, who sat on the hillside listening, seemed to be far away in memory
—memories of the wars they had lived through
in days gone by.

Then the bugles ceased and a long, clear
blast from the chief bugler gave the signal that
the race was now to be between Black Storm
who had led the field at the fairgrounds, and
the famous sorrel mare of the Major's.

Joe was ready; so was the Major. They rode
side by side toward the tape held, a little distance to the west, by two troopers. The General,
as elated as a youth at the prospect of the thrilling event, rode with them, saying, "Now, gen-

tlemen, remember! When the chest of each of your horses touches the tape I will fire my revolver. Each of you be ready."

"Very well, Sir," said the Major.

Joe Bain, looking at the General, nodded assent.

When Joe Bain and the Major, riding side by side, were within a dozen paces from the tape, and when the vast crowd was all standing on the hillside in breathless excitement, one of the troopers, holding one end of the taut tape, in his nervousness dropped his end. Just as he was walking forward to pick it up one of the strangest of the many dramatic happenings that ever occurred near Fort Riley, came—and came like a clap of thunder from a clear sky.

It was started by the wild, shrill scream of a boy.

In order that the thing may be fully understood, it will be well to tell of something that had occurred a little before. At Fort Riley in those days, several of the officers who were lovers of the chase kept some twenty-five wolfhounds, and day after day these fierce dogs might be seen trotting behind many mounted cavalrymen in the hills, or rushing like the wind across the highlands to bring down a wolf. There was one unfortunate thing about these dogs: if by chance any strange dog was sighted out in the distance with no man to protect him, they would race after the stranger and destroy him as quickly as they would a wolf.

It happened that about ten minutes before an officer had come riding up with a dozen or more of his big black and white wolfhounds, and had halted with his dogs a little west of the tape where the race was to start.

There was a boy in this throng of people who had ridden over in a wagon with his father to see Black Storm race. This boy, Don Henderson, owned a small, white collie, who had come along and, as was his custom, was at this moment hunting far up the valley.

All of a sudden now, the whole pack of wolfhounds shot out across the valley toward the small white collie, and Don, seeing them and knowing they had destroyed other dogs, uttered a piercing scream that made all eyes turn toward him.

"They'll kill my doggie! Oh, save my doggie!"

The officer who owned the hounds saw the danger and started at a run. On the same instant both Joe Bain and the Major saw and they, too, understood it all. The General likewise knew these hounds, and unless the dogs could be somehow overtaken the little white collie would surely be torn to pieces.

The small, white dog, looking up from his sniffing in a bunch of grass for a rabbit, saw the terrible demons coming and instinct warned him—he started to circle to get back to the boy. But he saw he never could do that, and crying in terror, he ran straight into the west over the hard valley sod as fast as his legs would carry him. But his collie leaps were pitiful compared to the giant leaps of the rushing wolfhounds. He had been far up the valley—fully a half mile away when the hounds started, and the plain stretched far and wide on all sides of him.

All this happened in a few flashing seconds.

The General and everybody forgot the race, yet now came that amazing race between Black Storm and the white-stocking mare—a race that could never have been fairer, for both she and Black Storm leaped away side by side. The General and a dozen of his officers came thundering on behind.

The little collie covered a quarter of a mile and still he was rushing on with the hounds eating up the distance between them.

A half mile, three-quarters; Black Storm and the mare ran neck and neck and then he passed her like a cloud moving across the face of the sun—and those riding behind saw Joe Bain swing low on his horse as he passed the first wolfhound. Joe lashed him hard in the face with his quirt, slowing the dog up. Another, and still another, and the big leader of the pack was almost upon the collie, reaching for him

with deadly fangs. Black Storm drew alongside
this foremost hound; Joe swung low and lashed
the big wolfhound with his quirt, then swinging lower still, he skillfully caught up the small
white dog behind the forelegs and swung him
up in the saddle while a half dozen of the big
hounds leaped for their intended victim.

As Joe did this he heard a wild, prolonged
cheer from hundreds of throats far down the
valley. All eyes had been looking, and men,
women and children understood the full meaning of it all. A terrible suspense had been felt
for the little white dog, and the boy had stood
in a wagon, wringing his hands and crying
while he looked.

The wolfhounds now, at the sound of their
master's voice, slunk away down the valley.

Joe Bain turned, and the Major riding up
on his hard breathing mare was the first man
to congratulate him.

"My mare is good, Joe," he said, "but Black
Storm is matchless. He has the greatest com-
bined speed and endurance of any horse I have
ever seen."

Joe rode back and deposited the small, white
dog in the arms of the boy, who was now laughing through his tears.

The great crowd thronged about Black
Storm. Civilians, troopers, officers, and the
women above all, had their eyes set upon the

great black horse. The mare stood apart, still breathing very hard, but oddly enough, although Black Storm had run farther than she, and certainly at a much faster pace, he did not seem to feel exhaustion. He was breathing a little heavily but he was breathing comfortably.

The General walked up and stroked him, patted his great shoulders, then moved around in front of him and looked with a critical eye at Black Storm's mighty chest.

"Bain," said the General, "you've got one horse in many thousands. If that horse were ever loose on the plains and had to run for his life from men riding to catch him, I'd wager he'd outrun at least three relays of fresh horses!"

"I hope he'll never be put to such a test, General," replied Joe, and when he said this he had not the slightest feeling that such a thing might come to pass. Yet oddly enough, the General's words were to prove prophetic.

When Black Storm finally left the valley that late afternoon with hundreds of admiring eyes upon him, Joe Bain had no suspicion of coming trouble.

It was night when he rode out on the broad Smoky Hill valley, lit by the summer moon and stars. Black Storm walked rapidly over the prairie sod, only his hoofbeats breaking the stillness of the night.

As Joe approached the trail leading up the high winding hill, he was aware of a horseman sitting his mount near a small tree on the plain. Joe pulled Black Storm up to a slow walk and watched the man like a hawk. He was relieved to hear the familiar voice of John McDonald.

"I've been waiting for you, Joe," McDonald explained. "I knew you'd soon be along the trail here. I want to tell you something while I think of it. Charlie says he has found out that there were two suspicious strangers at the fair when Black Storm raced and that one of them came to one of our boys last night and offered him a bribe to help steal Black Storm. It was Jim Patrick he tried to bribe. Jim cut him across the neck with his quirt for his offer and that was the end of that, but it means that you've got to watch that horse. I think you'll be safe if you'll make it a rule never to let him out of your sight when you leave the ranch with him."

"I'll do it, Mac," said Joe. "I'll admit I'm bothered a little but I won't even tie him in town while I go in a store. They can bring out what I want."

McDonald started his horse up the long cattle trail, and Black Storm followed; Joe rested his hands on the horn of his saddle, a new and troubled look upon his face.

## Chapter IV

### THE STAMPEDE

**D**URING the second week in June the worst rains of a generation began falling in the region of the John McDonald range. For more than two weeks the dreary, leaden clouds hid the sun and the watery heavens opened on the earth. What had been quiet, tinkling brooks in shady ravines suddenly became angry torrents, rushing and surging toward the streams of the Republican and Smoky Hill which joined here to form the Kaw River.

Day after day and night after night the rain fell, and day and night came the sounds of the water roaring down through deep cuts in the hillsides, while creeks and lesser streams, bank full, rushed on to pour their swollen torrents into the already rapidly rising Kaw.

During these days as Joe Bain rode up and down the wet valley around the nervous Longhorn cattle, he was always troubled—so were John McDonald and Charlie Bliss. They dreaded a stampede. Several times Joe had thought he would leave Black Storm at the stables and ride one of the small cow ponies but there were two reasons why he did not do this: first, in case of trouble no pony could take the place of Black Storm, and second Joe remembered the two strangers at the fairgrounds the day of the race. He wanted Black Storm with him.

Saturday afternoon came. The skies cleared and when the night fell, moon and stars shone down on a drenched world.

Five thousand head of new Longhorns had been driven under rainy skies from Abilene a week before.

This evening, as darkness came creeping over the earth, Joe Bain, on Black Storm, came riding fast to the home of John McDonald.

"Mac," he called as the big boss got up from the supper table, "the whole bunch of new cattle have worked down on the west bottom. They're awful restless, too. I've got some of the men down there trying to keep them quiet but there's a restless steer among them. The Smoky is up but the Kaw is up bad."

A troubled look came over McDonald's face. He got up from the table, mounted his horse and as the two swung away, he said to Joe, "We'll have to make a night of it, Joe. Maybe we can hold the cattle where they are and keep them quiet until morning. Then we can drive them back in the hills."

Bain and McDonald rode down in the valley to find the cattle restless, some of them already milling and all of them showing signs of great uneasiness, the main cause of it all being in the old brindle steer. He was nervous, restless, constantly moving.

More than thirty cowboys were riding around them using gentle words to quiet them and with the help of McDonald and Joe Bain the cattle finally were still; a few of them lay down, but not many. They were strung out in a long space up the valley, a few cattle lying here and there on the outskirts of the long line, the others standing in the center.

Around the whole herd the cowboys rode,

slowly and well apart, singing gently as they rode, for long experience had shown these cowmen that when the nervous Longhorns were held in the stillness of the night, the low crooning song of a man on a horse near by had a lulling effect on them. And so these cowboys, riding around these restless, anxious cattle on this ominous night, sang their weird, chanting songs, songs that no man knew who made them.

At times as the hours went by Joe rode near some of the other cowboys in his moving up and down the long line of cattle. As often as he did so and the bright moon revealed the black horse, the same question was always asked, "How is Black Storm tonight, Joe, is he nervous?" Joe's answer was likewise always the same, for although the horse showed that he was keenly alert, he was otherwise as calm as the rest of them.

The hour of midnight came—and went.

Often in the moonlight John McDonald held his watch close to his face and looked at the time. Hope grew in him that the cattle could be held quiet until daylight. They could then be driven back into the hills and held there. As the time passed, McDonald was still more hopeful, for although the main herd of the cattle would not lie down, they seemed quiet enough. The familiar figures of the slow-riding men, singing, were doing the work of bringing quiet.

Joe Bain, on Black Storm, rode far up and down the valley, often speaking kindly to the horse.

The moon was now high up in the heavens shining like a ball of silver on the scene in the valley. Now and then could be heard a gentle swishing sound as a rider rode through a patch of bluestem grass, drenching the horse's legs to his body as if he had been in the river; and now and then brief splashing sounds as a horse crossed a water-hole in the grass; then again, the rhythmical hoof-beats of the horses on the wild prairie sod. Save this, the gentle squeak of the saddles, and the low singing of the cowboys, the night was hushed and still.

One o'clock came. Then in the distance came another sound from the north. A sound heard by every man, one that cast a strange feeling of apprehension over them—the ever-increasing, ever-threatening roar of the river at the flood. It came now as a dull, steady booming sound, incessant, with now and then a louder roar as the flood waters battled with themselves.

Since a little after midnight, Joe Bain and John McDonald, in particular, had noted a sound made by the Kaw River, now bank full, sweeping all to destruction before it.

The time dragged on. Then two o'clock of this never-to-be-forgotten night came. John McDonald always remembered, for he had just

looked at his watch. All the men said afterwards
that they had heard no unusual sound, but pos-
sibly the cattle heard, for those that were lying
down got up. Some feeling, at least, had made
a new uneasiness among them. They stood still
enough but seemed to be in a tension.

Suddenly, as startling to these thousands of
Longhorns as if it had been a crack of thunder,
there sounded on the still night the sharp bark
of a coyote. A wildly running steer came charg-
ing down the hill and the coyote, as if evil possessed, kept up his sharp yap, yap in the gloom
of the night.

Unfortunately, just at that moment there
were no riders near the cattle at the north part
of the valley as these had for some time past
been lying down in perfect quiet while those
on the south had been restless, and John Mc-
Donald and the others had been riding near
these trying to quiet them. Joe Bain had ridden
to the extreme south end of the valley where
a small bunch of the steers were at that moment coming restlessly up to the main herd. At
the sounds of the wildly howling steer John
McDonald and his men whirled their horses
and started up the line, but there was no time
to stop it—no time for anything. At the sounds
of the coyote, the steers farthest north started
in that direction. It was like an electric shock,
so suddenly did it all happen. In less time than

it can be told, the thousands of cattle were running northward, plunging and bawling with a thunder of hoofs that shook the earth and one of the worst stampedes in the history of the west was on. There was only one way to stop it —ride hard to the front, head off the leaders, and by whipping and shouting at their heads, turn them back.

The whole valley was suddenly a bedlam of running, bawling cattle, plunging horses and hard-riding men.

Bain and McDonald rode desperately on the west flank to reach the leaders and turn them.

But the foremost cattle had a great start.

The same thing was in the minds of both men. Desperately, they urged their mounts, trying to cut in ahead of the leaders before they reached the river. The cattle were headed directly for the stream where the banks were fifteen feet high and now full to the level prairie with the flood.

The roar of the river now a mile wide, sounded sullen and sinister in the night. The sickly gleam of lights in old Fort Riley beyond the flood, only added to the gloom. The dark river was sweeping by, roaring, and tossing giant, up-rooted cottonwood trees on the face of the water. Great areas of driftwood rode down to be swiftly pushed asunder by the waters boiling up beneath. A small shed, the roof of a big barn, a farmhouse, all darker spots on the face of the river, came riding down. An empty rowboat, bobbing up and down like a chip, was grasped by the flood, spun around like a feather and flung with a dull, splintering sound against a huge driftlog. Another sound, farther down—a great splash followed by a roar as the waters cut in under a high bank, hurling tons of earth and gravel into the seething flood.

If some fearful thing of evil had chosen the ground for this stampede, it could not have been worse.

The Kaw River here swung at an angle across the valley to the high bluffs on the east and along the base of these bluffs the flood was rushing. Thus there was left a long stretch of level valley running to a point at the bluffs like the letter V, and the bluffs there were high and steep—no way for the foremost cattle to stop once they reached the yawning flood—and ten thousand cattle might rush in, to drown in that dark, monstrous maw, more than a mile wide.

The fear-crazed Longhorns were running with John McDonald and his thirty cowmen strung out in a line and riding desperately to reach the leaders and turn them, yet to a man knowing they could never cover that ground in time.

"Oh, Lord!" groaned John McDonald, "if only Joe on that horse was up!" And then he was aware of a black streak of a horse flying past him—and on, out of sight, in the dim distance to the north.

And McDonald leading, there came, strung out in a long line behind him, his hard-riding, spurring, lashing men.

"Joe'll never make it!" McDonald shouted, lashing his horse furiously, hoping against hope —and then he could see the river not far beyond.

In the meantime Joe Bain was riding furiously alongside the Longhorns trying to cut in ahead of the leaders. Black Storm thundered across the wet plain, his great muscles sending him like a shot over the valley, his mane and tail streaming in the night, his nostrils wide, his eyes ablaze with purpose, for he understood —understood and proved to the skilled Joe Bain that he knew what to do. On the instant Black Storm reached the foremost leader, he crowded the animal hard, laid back his ears and bit the steer savagely on the neck, still crowding him hard to the right. Bawling and swerving from this black terror of the night the steer turned yet more to the right and those behind blindly followed him—still Black Storm crowded and bit and turned him more and more while Joe Bain lashed the animal with his whip.

Suddenly John McDonald realized that he was riding in a wide circle, and then both he

and the men strung out behind were aware that
the eastward swing was leading them gradually
away from the river. The cattle had been
turned!—surely turned, but as yet they saw not
the thing that had turned them—saw only the
rushing cattle on the outermost part of the
circle, yet every man knew it was the black
horse that had shot past them. Then far down
on the valley, the vast herd was brought to a
wildly milling mass, and held by skillful men,
and only then was Joe Bain seen—seen standing
by a great black horse who dropped his head
low, heaving for breath. By turns the men came
up to dismount, briefly petting him, and heap-
ing dire maledictions upon any man whom
they might see try to abuse him.

At last, Charlie Bliss, the small, wiry under-
foreman came up and patted Black Storm affectionately. "Joe," said he, "you've got a
wonderful horse; all you got to do now's to
watch him and see that some of those myste-
rious strangers don't get hold of him."

"I'll be careful, Charlie," said Joe, himself
still breathing heavily from the exertion, "and
you boys will all help me. Guess we better
scatter out again, Charlie!" Joe said this quickly
as he mounted Black Storm. And both men
rode out on the west flank where the cattle
were again becoming threatening, surging out
a little from the milling mass.

## Chapter V

## THE STRANGER

*A*FTER the stampede of the Longhorns on the valley that night Black Storm was often the topic of conversation among the cattlemen. It was seen that he was not only a beautiful horse but a very valuable one also. And now if it happened that Joe Bain rode him into the town and tied him for a moment to go into a store he was sure to find a throng of men looking at the horse when he came out.

One afternoon when Joe stopped Black Storm in the street for a large crowd of his admirers to look at, Tod McHenry, a wealthy cattle owner, offered Joe a flat price of one thousand dollars for the horse, saying he would take a chance on riding him.

"He's not for sale," said Joe laconically.

For a time Joe sat on the horse to allow the men to look at him and also to answer their questions. Black Storm stood with his head high, after his manner, his eyes bright, his neck slightly arched in the beautiful curve in which he naturally held it, his sides moving easily under the saddle as he breathed and waited. At this time, as always since the day of the race, he wore his white bridle and breast collar, and likewise the black saddle blanket with the white border and the four polished metal stars in the corners, all of which added to his already striking appearance.

"Joe, you got him fixed up awful pretty," Tod McHenry remarked, letting his hand slide down the glossy neck. "You sure got him dressed fine!"

"There's nothing too good for him, Tod," said Joe.

"Does he ever try to pitch any more?" asked another of the men.

"Not with me," said Joe with a smile.

"How about the other boys at the ranch?"

Loud laughter came from a few of the McDonald cowboys, standing near and one of them shouted, "He throws every man as high as Gilroy's kite, but he's plumb married to Joe—and to Helen—pays no attention when she gets on his back!"

"And he'll let half a dozen kids ride him!" shouted another, "but he's shore got it in for the rest of us hombres!"

Standing among those in the rear of the crowd on this afternoon was a stranger who seemed to be careless and at ease. It was remembered afterward by two of the men that while he seemed to show no more interest than the others, he nevertheless had gotten from them the information that while Black Storm would allow no man to stay on his back, except Joe Bain, he was not vicious, and that with halter and bridle on his head, he had never refused to be led. But this was brought out in such a seemingly careless manner by the stranger that nothing was thought of it at the time, since all the men were asking questions about the horse. This question therefore seemed quite natural, and as strangers were always coming and going in these days, nothing was thought of it.

Tod McHenry, like everyone now, knowing of Black Storm's love for Joe, said, "Joe, suppose you get off of him and let the men stand around him in a circle. Then you walk off a distance and say nothing, but stand still and let's see what he will do."

"He'll run over us to get to Joe," said one of the McDonald cowboys warningly.

"He won't run over you," said Joe, "he's got too much sense for that, but I think he will get to me just the same."

Joe dismounted and leaving the reins on the saddle-horn slipped quickly through the crowd and stood alone a dozen yards away. Black

Storm looked at him wonderingly, instantly showing concern. He raised his head a little higher, looked at Joe and whinnied anxiously.

"I hate to do this," said Joe, looking lovingly at his horse.

Black Storm walked around the closed circle of men once or twice, looking for an opening to get through, the while he kept uttering sounds of anxiety. He pawed once or twice near the men, and then he stretched his head out in the crowd and started pushing through it, slowly, carefully, but through nevertheless— and the men gave way laughing.

"He didn't want to hurt anybody," said Joe as Black Storm came up and put his nose on his chest, "but he had to come through!"

At this moment one of McDonald's cowboys came riding up with the information to Joe that the long-anticipated herd of new Longhorn cattle was expected at Abilene that night and that McDonald had sent word for Joe to come.

Immediately Joe mounted, and with a wave of his hand toward his friends rode away to meet the new cattle and lead them, as was his custom, to the grazing ground in the hills to the east.

The stranger in the meantime hurried away and two hours later he and another man were sitting in a buckboard and driving rapidly west on the trail of Joe Bain and Black Storm.

## Chapter VI

### A THIEF AT ABILENE

*W*HEN Joe Bain reached the town he found that the new herd of cattle was already there. There was nothing now for him to do but wait until morning. There was no need for him to stay up, so, after a conversation with the men, he rode to the home of a friend where he arranged it so that he might sleep in the barn with Black Storm. The cattle town was full of mad characters and Joe did not leave the horse a minute. He ate a sandwich for his supper, put Black Storm in the stall of a vacant barn, gave him feed and water. It was about eleven o'clock that night when Joe lay down on some hay in a runway of the barn almost under the nose of his horse.

Black Storm reached his head across the manger and Joe fondly petted him and talked to him a little, then lay back in a comfortable position and prepared to go to sleep.

The barn was well on the outskirts of the town and there was complete silence about the place. From where Joe lay on his bed of hay he could see through a small open door well up in the barn. Moon and stars were shining on what seemed a peaceful world. From a far distance Joe could hear the faint barking of a dog, and now and then some uncertain noises, as it seemed, down on the main street of the town.

Joe was nearly asleep when again Black Storm reached over the manger and put his nose near Joe's face. Again, Joe petted and said, "Good-night, Stormy, time to go to sleep now." And then, scarcely knowing why he did so, Joe got up and moved carefully to one end of the barn where there was a small door hooked on the inside. Noiselessly he lifted the hook and as noiselessly opened the small door. He could see some distance, but nothing greeted his gaze but an old buckboard with a broken hind wheel, which he had noticed when he led Black Storm in the stable. As he looked, a crippled horse limped past a little beyond the buckboard, stopped to rest a little and again limped slowly on and out of sight among the dim shadows. There was a narrow belt of woods west of the barn and as Joe looked in this direction he gave a sudden start, for he thought he saw the quick movement of some form as it passed through the shadows there. Still, there had been nothing certain about it and as he looked for a time at the place he could see no sign of life at all. Then a little north of the wood he heard the sounds of a galloping horse, but since this was the common mode of travel in those days, he thought nothing of it, supposing it was perhaps one of the cowboys riding out of town.

As Joe stood looking out in the bright moonlight a collie dog came trotting past, stopped for a moment at the buckboard, sniffed it a time, then trotted on, when he passed from sight in the small belt of woods beyond. Joe heard a sudden rushing sound there, such as a dog might make running through the brush after a rabbit.

Again all was still. Joe turned to look at Black Storm. The moonlight streamed through the small open door onto the horse's head. He was standing with his head down, his eyes closed, resting peacefully.

Slowly and without the slightest noise Joe

pulled the small door shut and put the iron
hook in place through the staple. The main
door of the barn was locked on the inside and
Joe told himself that things were safe enough
and that he had made more trouble than was
necessary. He again lay down on his bed of
hay and closed his eyes, his thoughts on his
horse and the morning. There were no other
horses in the barn and Joe wondered if there
was a curry-comb and brush in the place, for
Black Storm must be perfectly groomed at daybreak. He would not ride him forth with any
spots on him. But perhaps there was a comb
and brush somewhere here; he would get up

early in the morning and attend to his horse so that he would be on hand to lead the cattle east at an early hour.

Gradually the world of men and horses passed out of Joe's mind and he fell into a deep sleep. Black Storm also was sleeping peacefully in the stall just across from the manger.

When Joe first became conscious he was aware of a tremendous throbbing in his head. Things seemed strange and unnatural, and at first he thought he was in a hideous dream. He moved his arms and at last got to a sitting posture while his head swam and things blurred before his eyes. As his vision cleared he was aware the dawn had come and then as if in a dream he saw that the barn door was open. An unusually sharp pain in his head came and he put up his hand to find blood. He got to his feet and stood, weak and trembling, holding with both hands to the front of the manger.

Pale, weak, sick, a mist came in his eyes—he knew now what had happened—he had been struck a blow on the head—and Black Storm was gone.

Once outside Joe moved, weaving and staggering to the house. Two of the McDonald cowboys saw him and came running up.

"Hurry, boys!" was all they could get out of him. "They've stolen Black Storm! Hurry! Hurry! Ride hard in every direction!"

## Chapter VII

### MAN, THE ENEMY

*M*ILE after mile, twenty—thirty—fifty, until he was so weary he could scarcely stand, Black Storm trotted rapidly. He was tied securely with his halter rope to the rear end of a buckboard in which two men sat, flicking the two driving horses with the whip to keep them at a fast trot.

When Black Storm's captors had come in the barn that night, after rendering the sleeping Joe Bain helpless, Black Storm had tried to battle against being taken out, for although he did not know why, he did not like these strangers and was afraid of them. But both of them were skilled horsemen and after a brief time they got him tied to the rear of the buckboard. Once Black Storm pulled back hard to get away, but the strong leather and rope held him helpless and when he felt his head violently jerked, as the buckboard lurched forward, there was nothing he could do but follow.

As the hours sped by he was given no rest, and although after the first twenty miles fresh horses were hitched quickly to the buckboard, Black Storm got no rest. Hour after hour he felt the merciless pull of the halter on his head until his exhausted muscles ached and pained so severely he could scarcely drag his feet forward. He wanted so much to be free from all this. Once started, however, he did not keep up the fight against being led, for, from the first, when he was a little colt and had seen what men wanted when they put a halter on his head, he had always allowed himself to be led. He obeyed because it did not hurt him.

At least three times the horses drawing the buckboard were exchanged for fresh ones and during three days and nights Black Storm was allowed only the briefest intervals of rest while he drank from some stream where the men paused for him to get water and eat a small feed of grain. Not once was he taken more than a few yards from the buckboard, and at such times both men held him.

As Black Storm traveled on he saw no one except the two men who sat in the seat of the light wagon. On the fourth night a thing happened that seemed for a moment might save him. The moon was up and shining brightly on the plains. The two men were driving near the woods of a river when suddenly they turned the two horses off into the densest part of the timber. Here they stopped, and leaping from the wagon, one of the men held his hands on Black Storm's nose to keep him quiet. The other man held his hands on the heads of the other two horses. A sound could be heard on the prairie to the east, and presently a lone horseman galloped hard past the river woods. After the rider had passed one of the men peered out from the edge of the woods.

It was Joe Bain in search of his horse. Black Storm could not see the rider who rode swiftly on. He could only hear the sounds of the galloping horse.

When the sounds of the hoofbeats had died away on the moonlit plain, the two men got into the buckboard, drove out of the woods, and turned off the trail, driving rapidly toward the southwest. On and on they traveled until the moon hung low on the western horizon and then they turned off sharply to the right and took to the cover of a heavily wooded gorge through which coursed a small stream.

Black Storm, now permitted to halt, stood with drooping head breathing hard and trembling from sheer weakness. When he saw the other two horses taken away from the buckboard he dropped down on the ground. Being utterly weary he wanted to lay his head down also but the halter rope was too short, and he let his head down as far as the rope would permit and tried to rest. The two men went a little distance away with the other two horses and for a time all was still.

Faint gray streaks were beginning to show in the canyon. A mother coyote, holding food in her mouth for her young, paused near the mouth of the gorge to look, then padded softly away and vanished in the early dawn. A badger, whose home was in a near-by hill, came out and for some time gazed down on the great black form of a horse, then went back to sleep on his comfortable bed. The gray light faded into brighter day and the trees of the canyon stood hushed in the early hour of morning.

There were low sounds of men's voices a little up the stream, but Black Storm was unmindful and his nose weaved slowly as the halter rope prevented him from resting his weary head.

## Chapter VIII
### BLACK STORM IS FREE

*B*EFORE it was full daylight the two men hitched their horses and started away with Black Storm and on the evening of the same day they sold him.

He was now in a country where he was not known—in the far southwest. And here man after man bought him only to learn that he could not ride him, and then once more Black Storm's sheer beauty and loveliness would bring a good price, and again he would be sold. He was shifted from place to place with the halter never being taken from his head. And many times after he had been purchased and those who bought him discovered—as they supposed—that he was an untameable outlaw, he was tied fast and cruelly beaten, and time after time, his feed was withheld from him, and he was given only water. Then again, while in this condition, men with spurs would mount him and try to ride him but no man could stay on his back. He threw them all and threw them quickly.

At last he was bought by a man by the name of Wilson who lived on a ranch in a region of high hills and deep canyons. It was the same thing here. The men of this outfit all leaped upon his back, and whipped and spurred him after their manner of riding bronchos—and Black Storm threw them all in his wild leaping and pitching. But the riding was all done in large corrals and he never had a chance to escape.

The owner of the ranch was angry because he had bought him, and confined him in a stall in the stable until he could sell him.

Here Black Storm was pitifully neglected. No one in this region, now knowing him, would buy him because no man could ride him. It never occurred to any of these men that it was the fearful cutting spurs and the stinging lash of the quirt that made the horse stand in mortal fear of them all. Nor were they all bad men. Some of them were, it is true. But they tried to ride Black Storm in the same way they rode all horses in those days.

So day after day, here, Black Storm was tied up by the head and many times he saw the whole day pass with only water to relieve him. And a number of times the water was forgotten. It was the loss of this which made him suffer terribly.

But it happened that after some days of his confinement here Black Storm found a friend. This was an eight-year-old boy, Ted Wilson, son of the ranch owner. Ted was small for his age and was not permitted to go about much near the horses, but when he first saw Black Storm the boy was attracted by his beauty, and then afterward, when he had seen how cruelly the men spurred and whipped him, Ted wanted all the more to come close to the horse and be friendly with him.

One morning after all the men had gone out on the range Ted went out to the barn, opened a side door and went along the long alley-way in front of the mangers until he came to the stall where Black Storm stood. He was standing with his head down very low when Ted came up in front of him, but he did not show alarm, and after looking for a moment at the boy Black Storm reached his nose over and whinnied. Ted reached out and patted him on the nose, then opened the narrow door to the stall. He boldly went in near the feedbox and dropped therein a big lump of brown sugar. Black Storm laid hold of it and as he munched it he turned his head toward Ted and kept uttering little friendly sounds. Ted stroked his neck and looked at his sides. There were swollen lumps and dried blood on them caused by the spurs of the men.

"Poor Blackie" exclaimed Ted, not knowing his name, and his lips trembled a little. "It's no wonder you buck with them," he said, "I'd buck too. It's awful the way they treat you."

Black Storm finished his sugar and held his nose down to the boy, closing his eyes while Ted held the great black head in his small hands and stroked it ever so fondly. He could see the long welts on Black Storm's shoulders where many stinging quirts had lashed him. And as the child held his hands on the horse's head a sudden idea came to him and childlike he acted at once on the impulse.

"Blackie," he said, while Black Storm held his head close, "I'm not going to let them hurt you any more. I'm going to let you loose and maybe some man will find you who will be good to you!"

Then with trembling fingers Ted stood on

the feed-box, unbuckled the big halter at the top, and it dropped to the ground. Black Storm raised his head, shook it a little, and with eyes wide, he turned and looked at the open door behind him, again turned and put his nose down to Ted with that low whinnying sound, and once more looked at the open door in the rear.

"Good-by, Blackie," said Ted, patting his head for the last time, "go on out, Blackie! Hurry, and don't let the men get you!"

Black Storm turned slowly and walked out. He stood with his eyes wide for an instant, then started west, first at a trot, then broke into a gallop and ran faster as he realized he was again free.

Ted ran to some outbuildings and looked. Far out on the range he saw Black Storm galloping, then all of a sudden he heard wild yells and the next moment he saw three of the cowboys running and spurring their horses toward him. Then two others topped a ridge and came in on the race yelling and lashing their horses to their topmost speed.

Ted stood, his hands gripping the corner of a shed, and his voice came tense when he said, "I bet they never catch him! I *hope* they can't." But he was troubled, for the sounds of the yelling increased and he knew that many men were now riding hard after the black horse

## Chapter IX

### A HEART-BREAKING RUN

*A*CROSS narrow valleys, up high, steep bluffs, down into brush and tree-covered ravines, tearing through vines and brush, and on and on, splashing across little creeks and draws, Black Storm outran the hard-riding men of the Wilson ranch.

Late that night he reached the foot of a hill where there was a little tinkling spring. Here he stopped, weak, trembling, listening, waiting.

All that night he rested by the spring and for several days thereafter. He grazed about the place, wandering not more than a quarter of a mile from it while he fed on the wild grasses of the plains. Then at last his loneliness for companionship led him into trouble. During these days near the spring, he had seen now and then on a distant hill some horses peacefully grazing, and one day toward evening one of the horses raised his head, looked in Black Storm's direction and neighed loudly.

After the horse on the hill had thus called to him, Black Storm walked restlessly about his feeding ground. Night fell and the silver moon came up to shine brightly on plains and hills. Black Storm would put his head down to the grass, bite off a small mouthful, then look eagerly toward the hill where he had heard the horse neighing. At last he could endure his loneliness no longer and started toward the distant hill—and danger, of which he did not know.

It happened this night that the man whose duty it was at the Bill Grimshaw ranch to remove the halters from certain of the horses and let them loose in the corral before he closed the gate, was late with his work. The horses were still tied in the corral and the man was just going to untie them and close the gate, when, seeing a large, black horse approach, he dodged behind a shed, hid and waited. The corral gate was open, a dozen horses were tied therein waiting impatiently for the man to come in and remove their halters. One of the horses saw Black Storm approaching, and whinnied in a friendly manner.

Black Storm came slowly up and paused at the gate. The horse whinnied again. Black Storm walked in, came up, rubbed noses with the horse and they both whinnied in tones of greeting. At this moment the man slipped out and swiftly shut the gate. He then climbed over the corral and removed the halters from the horses.

The next morning, when Bill Grimshaw and his men approached the corral, they saw a strange black horse. They went in the corral and closed the gate, then saw him take sudden fright and rush and plunge among the other horses in his efforts to keep away from any man who tried to approach him. The practiced eyes of Bill Grimshaw looked quickly at the prize, then he said:

"Boys, we got an outlaw and he's a mighty pretty one, but we've got to rope him before we can ride him."

For an hour Black Storm leaped and plunged and battled to keep out of their ropes, but at last a noose caught him, closed so tight around his neck that he fell still struggling, and when

he finally lay still the rawhide rope that held
his legs was so drawn and tight that pains shot
through his muscles. Both his hind legs just
above the hoofs smarted fearfully where, in his
struggles, the friction of the ropes had burned
him until he bled.

The other horses were all taken out and Bill
Grimshaw approached with a bridle. Black
Storm did not resist now, only lay still. The
bridle was put on him and the bit between his
teeth; carefully the ropes were cut from him.
Black Storm still did not move and lay for a
time with his head up, his nose close to the
ground. Then his legs burned and smarted so
much where the rope had been on him he
wanted to stand, and as he got up the men
surged back, thinking he would fight them. But
Black Storm stood quite still, assuming the
characteristic position he had that morning
when Joe Bain first saw him in the corral.

Bill Grimshaw was a good judge of horses
and when he saw Black Storm was quiet he
looked him over, still holding the reins of the
bridle. He saw instantly, as did every horseman who looked at him, that he was an unusual
horse both for color and beauty of build. But
Bill Grimshaw overlooked the thing that from
the first struck pain and terror to the horse's
soul—the sharp, jangling wheel spurs such as
Bill and all his cowmen wore on their cowhide

boots. They all stood looking at Black Storm for a while, then Bill said, "Bring in a saddle. Maybe we should have put it on before we let him up, yet if I don't miss my guess, he'll pay no attention to the saddle, but something's going to happen when the first man gets on his back."

"What makes you think he'll stand the saddle?" asked one of the men.

"The way he sets his eyes back," replied Bill. "I've seen one or two like that before. I may be mistaken about him not bucking the saddle off —but we'll see!"

Very, very slowly the man came up with the big saddle, as the other men stood tense, watching. Bill Grimshaw held the reins and stood close. Nearer and nearer still the cowboy came up—touched Black Storm with the saddle, paused a pulsating second, then slowly eased it in place up on his back. Another man approached slowly from the other side, and taking the cinch reached it half-way under while the other man met the hand half-way and pulled the cinch up slowly, very slowly, until it touched Black Storm. Surely he would leap now—but he didn't, nor did he move when the cinch was drawn tighter and tighter and tied to their satisfaction.

"All right," said Bill, slowly putting the reins over Black Storm's head. "No broncho about him! Somebody's going to know they been somewhere when they get on him—want to try him first, Bud?"

Bud Langley, a long, lean cowboy, one of the best riders, came forward. He gathered the reins, and not touching his foot to the stirrup leaped squarely in the saddle. Langley stayed on a full minute, spurring and whipping after his manner of riding. Black Storm threw him hard. And in less than a half hour he had thrown every man in the outfit. Now he was in a wild frenzy because of pain. The men had cut him fearfully.

Black Storm stood sweating and quivering after he had thrown the last man. Bill Grimshaw now came up.

"He's a real beauty, anyhow," said Bill. "Got great stuff in him. Tell you what we'll do! We'll put him in the little stall in the barn and keep him there a couple of weeks. If we don't give him any exercise and then cut down on his feed we can weaken him some, and he won't have so much endurance. Then Bud, or some of the rest of you can stay on him till he's whipped. Once one of you can do that we got a great horse."

So they took him away trembling, frightened, his sides and shoulders stinging and smarting from whip and spur, and they led him to the narrow stall in the stable.

All that day and that night and the next day and the next—through two miserable weeks, Black Storm stood, resting first one foot and then the other. Sometimes his head sank low and he uttered a long, sighing sound. At such times, when half asleep, his mind went back to a man who seemed very plain to him. This man had none of those painful, cutting, jangling things on his boots, and he had in his pockets and in his hands the sweetest things to eat. It had seemed so restful to have this man's hands on him and his voice had brought peace and a soothing quietness that took away all fear. There, with that strangely kind friend, no trouble ever came.

Black Storm often raised his head and looked hopefully when he heard human footsteps approaching outside, and always he longed to hear the familiar voice of the man he would never forget. And once when one of the men at a distance cleared up his throat, it sounded so much like Joe Bain that the horse raised his head quickly, his eyes suddenly shining, his ears moving back and forth with wild expectation—only to see another man enter the barn.

So through the days and nights Black Storm was compelled to stand in the narrow stall, so narrow he could not lie down in comfort because of his size. During all this time a certain

man who always wore the things of torture on
his boots brought feed and water to him. But
he always came in the barn through an alley-
way in front of Black Storm because he was
afraid to go in behind him. Yet there was no
need for the man to fear, for Black Storm was
never known to kick at a man and if a stranger
who had been caring for him for some time,
told him to move either this way or that, he
tried to do what they wanted him to do—if they
would only give him a chance. He seemed to
have a fear of this particular man and when
he brought in feed and water Black Storm
moved back as far as his rope would allow, yet
the man always spoke to him quietly.

Then one day, just at the noon hour, the man
came in the stable and came so quietly he was
not heard. It happened at the time that Black
Storm, to ease his cramped muscles, was paw-
ing the ground a little below his feedbox. Without the least warning then, although the cow-
hand did it thoughtlessly he shouted, "Stop it!"

In mortal terror Black Storm lunged back;
the rope snapped and his momentum carried
him with a crash through the frail pine door
in the rear. He fell to his haunches, half outside, lunged clear out, got to his feet and started
at a run. A dozen men, hearing the crash, came
quickly out of the door of the ranch house.

Straight toward the west there was a wide,

open plain that lay for two miles, slightly broken here and there by rolling ground, between which were small gulches and draws. Out on this open ground Black Storm ran with all the power of his stiffened muscles. He heard the wildest of yells behind him, and presently, as he ran, he saw that he was pursued by many mounted men. In a frenzy of fear he put all his power into the running, but run as he would, he found that at the end of a mile his pursuers were gaining on him. His long confinement in the narrow stall had so cramped his muscles that they would not at once respond with their old-time power.

Black Storm did not know it, but it was this first, violent burst of speed that was hardest on him. And likewise he had no way of knowing his marvelous endurance which was far above that of all the horses pursuing him—if only he could have time to limber up. He knew only that his enemies were gaining on him and that he was mortally afraid of them.

At the end of another mile the plain dipped sharply and two low ravines loomed ahead, beyond which lay a long line of bluffs and ridges. Down the incline Black Storm ran and on up the first bluff-side. He reached the summit of the hill ridge and found that some of his enemies had reached it first, but some distance on either side of him, while others were running and yelling in his rear. Straight down the low bluff on the other side Black Storm ran to another open plain, and again he headed straight west while his pursuers on either flank spurred and lashed their mounts frantically in an effort to cut him off.

Black Storm raced across a quarter of a mile of level grass land, then shot up a long incline, and with this his muscles began to respond. With his blood now hot, his old power began to come into him. Three riders on either side, nearest to him, lashed their mounts furiously to cut in ahead of him and turn him back, but Black Storm not only held his own but slowly and surely increased his lead.

Knowing the lay of the land perfectly, Bill Grimshaw sought to turn him by strategy. Mounted on a good horse himself he yelled to two of his men who were unusually well mounted. These three swerved off from the running in the rear, and lying low on their horses' backs, whipped and spurred their mounts into the perfect cover of Powder Gulch, a long, deep cut, the bottom of which was dry and hard. Bill Grimshaw shot into the gulch first and the other two men came riding in hard behind him.

This gulch was bordered on either side with tall, thick-set bluestem grass and sumacs, and the three men riding hard below were completely hidden while driving like the wind at an angle toward the black streak of a horse running almost straight west.

A fearful mile Bill Grimshaw and the two men rode through the gulch and now as they neared the end Bill stood up in his stirrup and saw the black horse less than a hundred yards away. With a yell of triumph the man struck his horse with his quirt and shot out of the cut, as he did so working frantically with his lariat rope.

Black Storm saw; he whirled so sharply he almost fell and barely escaped the whirling noose of Bill Grimshaw. At this moment an unexpected thing happened. Two cowmen from the West range topped a rise of ground directly in front of Black Storm. Instantly the two riders saw it all, and jerking their lariats from their saddles came bearing straight down toward the black horse. For a moment Black Storm was almost surrounded but he never hesitated. The two men in front, sweeping down upon him, supposed he would do what the average horse would do, try to run either to the right or left of them. Accordingly, the two men separated a little so that no matter which way he turned one of them would intercept him and turn him back toward the other rider. But instead of veering off either to the right or the left Black Storm shot like a thunderbolt straight on and before the astonished men could realize it, he flashed between them and was racing like a streak in the clear. Wild yells of disappointment smote the air and the whole field came riding in hard behind him.

At the end of that heart-breaking run of many miles, the men pulled up at the buildings of the West ranch, horses completely spent, groaning and struggling for breath. They jerked off the saddles, threw them on fresh horses, and again raced on after the now distant black spot on a plain to the west. Again they gained on him and again Black Storm, groaning with the effort, put on speed and held his own, bearing now toward the north, for there, in the distance, he saw trees and wooded bluffs which seemed to beckon him in his distress.

The day was at a close and the dusk of evening was fast coming over the land. With heartbreaking sobs Black Storm thundered on with his pursuers still spurring and yelling after him. His once beautiful black coat was covered with sweat and foam, the whites of his eyes were bloodshot, his nostrils were wide and fiery red with his heaving struggles for breath, and something like fire was shooting through his chest and brain. His black mane and tail were still streaming in the wind, his hoofs still struck the sod with a clatter so rapid they sounded like muffled musketry; and still with only his heart to bear him up, he ran on another mile, and still on toward the hills while to the astonishment of the men behind him, their fresh mounts now began to slacken in their speed in spite of spur and quirt. Then just as the darkness closed, by the most desperate efforts, they spread out on either side and Black Storm, still running straight on for the nearest cover—a cover he supposed would be friendly to him—he rushed through the thickets and trees of what was known as the Pocket Canyon.

Bill Grimshaw dismounted as did all the others. "Did you ever see anything like it?" said Bill, himself breathing hard like the rest of the men. "Well," he continued, "some of you get back and bring up fresh horses. You know he can't get out of the Pocket here and he'll have to get out here if he gets out at all. We'll keep up a watch until morning and hold him in. And then with all fresh horses he can't get away. If I get my hands on that horse again I won't take a thousand dollars for him, and this time I'll get him! If I thought it necessary, we'd build a fence across this end and take our time about running him down in the Pocket but it will be easy when daylight comes. He'll be stiff and still dogtired. We'll mass close and cover the opening and some of us will ride up in the canyon and rope him as soon as it's good daylight."

## Chapter X

### CAUGHT IN POCKET CANYON

WHEN Black Storm ran into the Pocket Canyon he was so weak his legs would scarcely bear him up. Quivering like a leaf he stood leaning against the steep side of the canyon for a time until his breath came, then struggled on in the darkness until he came to the high precipitous wall that blocked him completely. A thin stream of water was pouring down over the cliff, making a low roaring sound as it fell into a shallow pool below.

Black Storm was parched with thirst but the fear in his heart, that he was trapped, for the time drove all else from him. He walked along the cliff, splashed through the shallow pool, then moved down along the wall of the canyon looking for a place of escape. He knew his enemies were waiting and watching for him down at the end of the canyon for their loud shouts and calls came to his ears. Once he thrust his hot nostrils into the small stream, gulped a few mouthfuls of water and again hurried a little up and down searching for a place where he might get up and away.

At last he walked rapidly about on the stones and gravel—he was aware that he heard no sounds below him. Fearful and uncertain, he stopped and looked down in the darkness. He longed to rush down the canyon and run for the open, but his reason told him his enemies were still there—and he was so weary now—he could not escape them.

As he stood by the stream, waiting and listening, he thrust his head down time after time to gulp quickly a little water, but only a little, then again stood tense, watching. Were they coming in after him? This feeling worried him constantly.

Once Black Storm started violently, for he thought he heard them quite near and a little above him. He looked up and in the shadowy night saw a wolf that came out of some thin bushes near the top of the canyon. The wolf stood plainly revealed in the moonlight, but after one look the horse paid no attention to him and again looked anxiously down the canyon.

After some time, seeing no sign that the men were coming any nearer and hearing no sound from them, Black Storm dropped his head and tried to get ease from his exhaustion. His knees trembled and he wanted so much to lie down, but for some time he fought against this. At last, however, he dropped to his knees, and slowly went down on his side, drew a long breath and lay very still. His eyes were closed but he did not go soundly to sleep; his brain was still awake and listening. There was almost complete stillness everywhere now, yet to him it was a warning stillness. Black Storm did not know what the men were doing on the plain before the mouth of the canyon—he only knew that they were there, for now and then the faintest of sounds came to him from the distance below, sounds, faint though they were, that caused him to pause in his steady breathing, open his eyes wide, and look.

If Black Storm had been hidden nearer the mouth of the canyon he would have seen at different points on the plain many riders with ropes on their saddles, each rider standing beside his horse. Some of the men were holding the reins of their mounts while the horses fed on the grass, while others were carefully examining the cinches of their saddles, preparatory for the rush if the black horse should try to come out of the canyon. It had been planned that at daybreak two of the men should ride in and try to rope him. But they were all watching closely now, for fear he might try to slip out during the night.

The men were spread out so that they formed

a large half circle and it was impossible for Black Storm to come out without running afoul of some of them. Then, as a double precaution, some men had taken places well behind those at the mouth of the canyon. All the horses had been badly jaded by the record-breaking run of the afternoon, but new horses were steadily brought up as the night dragged slowly past, and new riders also kept coming in, all on fresh horses.

Expert horsemen were those who waited and watched with lariats for Black Storm.

In the meantime, well up in Pocket Canyon, with its many clumps of bushes and stunted trees, Black Storm lay, so weary and exhausted his head seemed to grow heavier and heavier. It sank lower and lower and at last he dropped it down prone to the ground to rest on a little patch of shale. Here he now lay sound asleep. For many minutes he did not move, but lay as still as if he were dead. Moon and stars looked down in the sober hush, and for a time there was no sign of life save the regular breathing of the black, foam-covered sleeper.

Black Storm slept for fully four hours. Then he leaped to his feet in an instant. A number of the riders below had fired at a prowling coyote and the roar of the big Colt's revolvers came booming up the canyon to strike terror in Black Storm. He whirled about and trotted

straight up the canyon until he came to a point
where he had been before, but this time he did
not pass it by. On the contrary he looked up
the steep which now lay plainly revealed in the
bright moonlight.

Up this steep was a most dangerous trail, if
trail it might be called. It led up over white
rocks and here and there very small bushes
whose roots clung uncertainly in the tiny crev-
ices of the ledges.

Black Storm was desperate. He leaped up to
the first flat ledge, some three feet across. From
this rock he worked his way laboriously up and
still up, once threading his way up a most
dangerous ledge—one so narrow his great body
touched the precipitous wall while his right
front foot was set down half-way over the edge.
A piece of rock fell to the depths below.

Black Storm was now frightened at his dangerous position. He could not turn back. He
stretched his long neck out and looked fearfully
at the dangerous depths below him. He was
fully two-thirds the distance up toward the top
of the canyon. He could not go farther, for the
ledge before him veered off treacherously into
the high wall of rock which formed the end of
the Pocket.

Slowly, half dragging his hind hoofs to feel
the ledge, Black Storm backed down, backed
and hugged the side of the cliff, crowding so

hard he left some of his hair on the rough rocky wall. And still backward he moved, his steps so slow, so careful, and time after time he paused to rest under the strain. At last he once more stood on a wide rocky ledge. He did not become panic-stricken but turned slowly, ever so slowly, and once more he was headed back on the uncertain trail. It was harder going down than coming up. He was a long time threading his way down and many times he stopped and felt with a front foot to make sure of his footing.

At last he stood again on the bottom of the Pocket and once more he walked down to the patch of shale where he had for a time rested.

After standing awhile and listening he again felt the need of more rest and once more he slowly went down on his knees, then at full length, and once more he dared to close his eyes and sleep. But now it was always a troubled sleep—a sleep that was almost constantly broken by sudden bad dreams when he seemed to be running with many men riding hard behind him.

Yet he remained in his prone position, remained and waited and tried to rest. He knew that when the morning light came he would have to fly from his enemies for he heard, again and again, the sounds of their voices.

They would not go away. They were waiting for him.

## Chapter XI

## THE RUSH FOR GOOSE CREEK WOODS

THE first streaks of the dawn were breaking when Black Storm quickly got to his feet. He shook his great black body, making the dirt and small particles of shale fly from him, then stood tense for a moment, his ears cocked forward, looking down toward the mouth of the canyon. He could not see far enough through the scattering trees on the floor of the gorge to make certain his enemies were there, but something warned him that they were, for now and then came to his ears distinct sounds of the men's voices.

Black Storm walked to the edge of the narrow stream and drank nervously. Again he raised his head and looked down through the gray light toward the mouth of the Pocket. A long breath came from him, like a sigh. He sensed the truth that again he must run as he had before. And now with both ears cocked stiffly forward, he started toward the only way out. At first he walked slowly and looked searchingly before him. Nearer and nearer he came, still hidden by the tall thickets and trees, until he stood behind a clump of bushes through the tops of which he could see the half circle of mounted men, and well behind them, more than a score of others in every direction, waiting for him on the plain.

In view of what happened here, a thing that the men who took part in it never forgot, it will be well to describe the lay of the land near the mouth of Pocket Canyon. The mouth of the canyon faced almost directly north; on the east and north was a plain, mainly level, that stretched away for many miles. Not far to the west there coursed what was known as Goose Creek, bordered on either side by a wide fringe of elm and cottonwood trees with much underbrush and trailing vines. Goose Creek, at this point, was a narrow stream, but deep and swift with its ever muddy and turbulent waters. To the west of Goose Creek there lay a vast stretch of rough land of high hills and narrow valleys covered for the most part with timber and scrub.

As Black Storm looked through the highest twigs it was light enough to see clearly the lay of the land before him—he saw the open plains, to the left and not far distant, the woods of Goose Creek—and his enemies—ready. Did Black Storm plan, in the brief moment that he stood watching from the thicket, how he would run for his freedom? That can never be answered for certain, yet there were those who saw who believed he did.

The west side of the Pocket, toward the Creek woods, was unusually well guarded, there being now fifteen men at that point, sitting their mounts with lassos ready. The main body of the men was stationed in single file so as to guard the gap on the north and east while half a dozen more sat their horses a little back and north of these. One thing is certain: Black Storm, when he started out, picked the place in the line to break through.

It was not yet quite broad day but light enough, as has been said, so that men and horses could be seen distinctly. The two picked men were just starting into the Pocket, when, without the slightest warning, Black Storm shot out from the bushes of the Pocket and into the open.

There arose a wild yell, "There he comes!"

Like a meteor flashing through the heavens, Black Storm raced out and without an instant's hesitation whirled away to the northeast. Pandemonium broke loose on the plain and thirty men rushed hard to get upon him. So suddenly had he rushed, and with such astonishing speed, he was almost upon the nearest men before they could get in action. The two foremost riders spurred in toward him, at the same time sending their long lariats hissing through the air to rope him.

Black Storm knew the danger; he came thundering down as if to break through the circle, but when almost within reach of their ropes he swerved sharply to the east. As he rushed out in that direction the men bore down upon him whirling their coiled lariats, while other riders rode guardedly well behind them. Surely, they thought, some of the nooses must get him now, but again, with scarcely a check in his rush, he whirled and ran northward and with such a burst of speed he left those on the right behind him, while he had shortened the distance between him and those on the west. Two riders on this wing, swinging their lariats, came driving in like the wind. Now, both these men were within distance and their treacherous

ropes shot out. At that instant Black Storm upset all calculations. They supposed if their
ropes fell short that he would whirl back and
so still remain in the circle and again the whole
field would have a chance, being around him.
But Black Storm had his own plan. Knowing
as he must have known, that now was his only
chance, he stopped and whirled so sharply that
both nooses fell on him, but slid harmlessly
across his back to drop to the ground. Black
Storm shot between the two riders, so close that
he knocked one cow pony staggering, while
bearing with crushing force against the man's
leg, leaped clear and ran for the woods of
Goose Creek.

Loud, angry yells rent the air as all the riders
bore in after him. Across the plain with all his
power Black Storm ran for the woods, reached
them, crashed through the outermost brush,
plunged headlong through the thickets and
vines, floundered on the steep, muddy bank,
fell on his side in the water, struggled up and
plunging in the stream swam with powerful
strokes until he was across. When his feet struck
the opposite shore, he lunged out of the water
and on through the woods to the timber and
scrub in the hills. And still on he ran, down
little bluffs, leaping narrow draws, splashing
through low bogs, and on along grassy lanes,
through sumacs and bluestem until he reached

a low dip between two high bluffs. Here he flattened out and ran hard, his head outstretched, his nostrils distended, his black mane and tail flying; and the voices that he had heard behind him now died away to a faint echo. But Black Storm, remembering only that he was free, ran on and on and on.

At last, only trotting—then walking and often stopping to rest—it was sunset when he splashed across a little creek, drank a few mouthfuls of water and halted. His head hung low, his sides rose and fell rapidly, but he did not stand long here; as the darkness began creeping over the earth he started away, not knowing where he was going, yet being led by something in his brain that kept telling him of one good man now far away. And blindly he walked on, not knowing how to find this man yet knowing by some instinct that the direction lay eastward. Black Storm could not tell that it lay exactly east, but the homing instinct made him know that he must move in that general direction. So he turned to the east and, walking slowly, started back on the long home trail. If he could have held to a course almost directly east, he would have finally come directly to the Mc-Donald's cattle range.

After traveling for an hour he halted on the edge of a little grassy draw and here in the tall, wild grass he lay down and rested until nearly

morning, then once more got to his feet and
started as best he knew in the right direction.
But fate was not kind to him, for, instead of
traveling straight into the east, he moved steadily a little south.

It was now November and while this fall had
thus far been mild, the storms of winter were
coming. In the evening of that same day as
Black Storm traveled on, a great angry cloud
rolled swiftly up from the northwest and a cold
wind arose that chilled him. Instinct warned
him to seek shelter and he broke into a gallop.
A storm was coming and so was the night, and
both were coming fast.

## Chapter XII

# IN THE WILDS OF A SAVAGE WINTER

**W**HEN the night fell it came so black that Black Storm could not see a dozen paces ahead of him. With the coming of darkness the wind whipped down hard from the north and a fine mist began driving down, changing within less than an hour to a heavy downpour of rain. In much anxiety Black Storm galloped rapidly across the plains. He wanted shelter from the cold, driving rain, yet there seemed no place where it might be found. He turned, his head away from the storm and ran with it toward the south.

As he galloped on, the night grew colder and colder, and presently, mingled with the rain, there was sleet that began freezing everywhere on his black coat and chilling him to the bone.

He ran until he was breathing hard, but still there was no shelter. At last he stopped just under the brow of a steep knoll that only slightly broke the wind, and turning away from the driving, wet sleet and rain, he held his head low, bunched all his feet close together and stood still while shivers ran through every part of him. At times he shook his head with the misery of it all but there was no use to run away from the hillock—it was only worse on the level plains. The icy water ran in streams down his sides and legs, and then as the night grew steadily colder there came only the sleet which quickly froze on his back, his sides, his legs, his head, even his ears, and he kept struggling with his eyes to keep them open for the ice was trying to freeze on his eyelashes. At last he could stand it no longer and again started out, running before the knifing storm. A fine frozen sleet drove down upon him, in hissing, rushing blasts, cutting and stinging like a million jabbing needles.

Black Storm was galloping hard when out of the black night there loomed a yet deeper blackness and he ran pell mell into some brushy woods where it happened that a large herd of Texas Longhorn cattle had taken refuge. The cattle broke a little as Black Storm rushed upon them, but seeing only a horse they quickly crowded close together again. Black Storm pushed into the woods as close to them as they would permit and here he stood and shivered and suffered with the cattle. As the hours dragged it grew bitter cold and morning came on a white, frozen world.

As soon as it was light Black Storm saw something that instantly frightened him. Many cowboys were riding across the sleet-covered ground from the east toward the herds of Longhorn cattle, which had strayed in the storm from the Sweet-Brier ranch.

Black Storm whirled and ran out of the woods across some rolling ground toward the west, galloped up to the top of a high knoll, then stopped to look back.

Unfortunately, a dozen men in this outfit had, before this, seen Black Storm and they recognized him instantly. Knowing, as they did, the impossibility of catching him on ordinary horses, one of the men jerked his rifle to his shoulder and as Black Storm stood looking, the cow man fired, hoping only to "crease" him. To "crease" a horse in these days meant to fire so accurately that the ball would only graze the top of the neck and so stun the horse for a little that he might be captured. The truth was that in this attempt at creasing, more horses were killed than were captured alive, for the ball, only too often, might strike too low—in a vital spot.

Black Storm had known nothing of firearms up to this time and had been, as he supposed, standing at a safe distance as he looked from the top of the knoll. For a moment he had stood there, a majestic creature with his head held high, his tail slightly uplifted, his eyes wide.

Then came the streak of fire.

The bullet struck him glancingly in the flesh near his withers and the shock of it, while it knocked him to his knees and sent blinding flashes before his eyes, did not render him unconscious; after the first brief second he leaped to his feet, whirled toward the west and ran as he had never before run in his life, the cowboys pushing in behind him with all the speed in their smaller horses.

For a brief time they pursued him and on coming to a rough region of low bluffs and ravines, they tried all the tricks they knew to out-maneuver him and so cut in ahead and turn him eastward, but Black Storm ran straight west—and westward still, his brain in a whirl, his soul stricken with terror. In less than twenty minutes he had left them all far away.

All that day and until far into the night, he hurried westward, sometimes slowing down to a walk, at other times swinging into a brisk gallop, and now and then stopping to drink when he came to a small ice-covered creek in the center of which was a narrow lane of dark water. None of these streams were deep and Black Storm plunged across them, breaking through the ice, with the water coming up to his knees. It was near midnight when he stopped in the darkness of a heavily clouded night. Terror was still in his heart but he was now very weary.

Here he lay down at the foot of a low bluff where the wind had blown the ground bare of sleet and snow. He tried to doze and rest but in his state of mind there was no rest for him and he could only wait for the night to pass. A bitter, cold wind whipped down from the north to send rushing blasts of sleet howling and moaning across the wild plains. Shivering and still too weary to travel, Black Storm got to his feet and again he stood trying to rest. At the end of another hour he once more started toward the west.

After a time the daylight came but he had no mind to change his direction. From this time on he traveled many days, and parts of many nights, as he still moved westward.

All the reason Black Storm possessed had been driven out of his brain by the constant feeling that behind him somewhere was the man with the long deadly black thing that spat fire and awful pain. So, driven on by this constant fear, he moved farther and farther into the western wilds. He knew not where he was going except that he was fleeing from the danger and pain.

Finally he reached a point near the foothills of the mountains and here he remained. There was enough withered buffalo grass to sustain him, but as the days went by the bitter cold, his constant anxiety, his loneliness and his helplessness, all helped to eat in on his body and spirit. Yet here he existed for many weeks.

One bitter cold night, when it was nearly morning, he entered some pine woods at the foothills of the mountains for shelter. He was now very thin, his hair stood on end, his eyes were sunken and suffering was written in his face. He moved in among the pines and had rested in the darkness for a time when suddenly he threw up his head, turned and stood with wide, frightened eyes looking out into the gloom of the night on the plain. He heard sounds borne down on the moaning wind, sounds weird, wild, deadly—the howls of timber wolves. They were coming down from the north where the long line of foothills fell away from the mountains to the rolling plains.

Black Storm stood tense, listening. The sounds were coming nearer, sweeping down the edge of what was known as Grizzly Gulch at the edge of the level land. The beasts had struck Black Storm's trail, a huge lobo wolf and three of his pack. Black Storm's instinct told him the

truth and his first feeling was to stand and battle with the wolves for his was a spirit proud,
courageous, defiant. Yet as he stood listening
another feeling came—a warning to run from
these deadly enemies, and acting on this he
leaped out of the shelter of the pines and ran
along the open plain, keeping near the line of
trees as he ran.

Black Storm was in no condition for this effort that strained his every muscle. He did not
exert himself to his utmost and turned his head
from side to side to look back, blowing loudly
through his nostrils, his proud, defiant spirit
filling him more and more with the fire of
battle. This was not the first time Black Storm
had heard the howls of gray wolves, but always
before he had heard them in company with
many other horses while he was sheltered in
the stables or sheds of the ranches where he had
lived.

Now it was different. He was alone in the
wilds of a savage winter night. Instinct told him
to run and he did so—out on the open plain
beyond the foothills. He ran hard, fearfully
hard, but the beasts behind him were deadly
at this. As Black Storm ran he felt his strength
failing. Daylight had come; at the same time
the howls of the timber wolves drew nearer and
nearer. He was desperate now and swerved to
the right into some timber and scrub. He

plunged through drifts up to his knees among the low thickets and crossed the wide belt of scrub to the open plain beyond, only to find that his cunning pursuers had taken the advantage by running around the lower end of the thickets, and then up the east side in the clear. By doing this they had run swiftly while he was leaping and almost floundering through the brush and drifts of snow.

When Black Storm surged through the thickets and brush into a long stretch swept almost bare of snow, he started to run east but saw the three wolves with the lobo in the lead already running in a circle around him. Raising his head high against the driving northern wind, his eyes blazing, his great heart throbbing, Black Storm stamped the ground and uttered a wild, shrill neigh, his bugle blast that the fire of battle was in him. He leaped and ran so swiftly toward the foremost wolf that the beast barely swerved aside in time to escape his sharp, deadly striking forefeet. But Black Storm stopped with amazing quickness and again he was upon the wolf. The beast leaped aside, and as he did so Black Storm's front hoof struck him a blow that sent him sprawling. At that instant the lobo and the two others rushed in to slash and hamstring Black Storm, and they missed him only by inches as he kicked like lightning and whirled to meet them.

## Chapter XIII

## A BATTLE WITH TIMBER WOLVES

OLD Lou Williams, the grizzled hunter and trapper of the Pine Creek region of Colorado, threw down his gloves in disgust after trying in vain to release a jammed shell in his gun while the temperature was 20° below zero. At last he gave it up, and bemoaning his luck, pulled on his gloves, began beating his arms about him to warm his stinging fingers. He had decided to go back to camp to remove the shell from his rifle. As he stood beating his arms old Lou looked beyond him at a certain big lobo wolf's tracks on the snow,—tracks that he had been following all morning through a lonely stretch of forest at the eastern edge of the mountains. A little to the right of the man the hills sloped down to the plains on the east.

It happened at the moment that Lou stood well up on the hillside where the trees were small and scattering. He picked up his rifle and was about to proceed on the back trail when he jerked up his head and his eyes opened wide in astonishment.

Below him on the open plain stood a black horse and circling him slowly with deadly intent were the big lobo wolf and two others. As old Lou looked, he saw the lobo rush in like a shot and slash at the horse's hamstrings. Black Storm, his eyes blazing, his muscles tense, kicked like the strike of a rattlesnake, struck the shoulder of the low-charging wolf, upset him, whirled and was almost upon him with striking four hoofs when the others, taking advantage of this, drove in his rear. Again came the lightning-like kick and this time a sound of the impact of his hoofs fair against the foremost wolf and before the beast could recover Black Storm was upon him, striking him, leaving the wolf limp upon the snow. The lobo rushed, slashed for the hamstring, ripped through the skin, but Black Storm, with flashing quickness, kicked and caught the lobo with terrific impact—the big beast, with a broken shoulder, went down with a snarl, his ears laid flat to his head, his fangs bared. He struggled up on three legs, when the horse whirled, and both his hind legs shot out like steel springs; one hoof struck the big wolf fair on the head, crushing his skull and knocking him ten feet into a dip in the frozen snow.

On the instant Black Storm whirled and leaped for the other wolf; it beat a retreat and ran toward the woods along the foothills. Black Storm again whirled expecting another attack from the rear, but he saw that the two gray beasts lay still in the snow. He stood for a moment blowing hard through his nostrils and looked at the running wolf. At this instant old Lou Williams, who had again been working frantically with his gun, got out the jammed shell, reloaded, jerked his rifle to his shoulder and fired. The fleeing wolf tumbled backward down the slope. At this, the black horse, with a new terror in his heart, shot away over the snowy wastes to the east, running as hard as his half-starved body would permit; while old Lou, hurrying as fast as his legs would let him, got down on the level, only to see the horse disappear in a depression a mile away.

Williams stood looking about him on the gloomy plain. He looked now at the dead lobo, then at the other and lastly at the snow-covered ground. All around on that little plain there were many tracks of the horse and the gray wolves—and the trails of all leading here from the south.

"By Jove!" exclaimed Williams after he had looked for some time. "They've run that horse and run him until he came to a stand here. The three brutes had spent hours here trying to hamstring him before I came up and he's been too quick for them. Thunder!" exclaimed old Lou, straightening up and looking eastward, "he looked awful poor and thin—must have strayed and got lost from somebody—wonder how he lives in all this. Got stuff in him—that horse has—wonder how he lived here."

And then as Williams walked on toward the north, near the edge of the woods he read the answer to his question. In many places here he saw where the horse had pawed the snow from the buffalo grass and a little farther on he came to a small stream fringed with cottonwoods. He saw that the green twigs of these had been eaten off for a considerable distance on either side of the creek.

"I see!" said old Lou, standing and musing to himself. "He's been here for weeks, picked out

this place and tried to live for the winter because it was close to the woods and he could go
in there during storms. A mighty sensible horse,
that—too smart for those dangerous beasts. I'm
sorry I scared him—he seemed terribly frightened when I shot—didn't quit running at all—
*terribly* scared. I wonder if anybody ever shot
him—he ran like it. But the man who would
shoot at that horse would be a fool. Thunder!
He killed the old lobo! Confound the luck—
much as I want that wolf, I'd rather he'd got
away if I could have got that horse. I don't
reckon there's a chance that he'll ever come
back here now, and I hope he can live 'til the
grass comes again. It's March, now, maybe he
will."

Old Lou walked slowly back along his trail
to remove the pelts of the wolves and again
he stood on the ground where the battle was
fought.

In the meantime, Black Storm was far away.
He was in terror because, to him, the man he
had seen was a mortal enemy. At last, having
run until he could run no longer from the thing
that spit the deadly fire, he halted in a low
gulch. He was now only a shadow of the horse
that Joe Bain had known on the McDonald
range. His ribs and hip bones protruded fearfully, his once beautiful sleek coat was long
and harsh. Only that arresting fire that still

burned in his luminous eyes told of the unconquerable spirit in him.

After he had breathed a little he started on, walking toward the east.

It is probable he remembered that men were somewhere in this direction—men that he must avoid at all odds; but it is even more certain that he knew, and had known since that night he was taken away, that there was one man in that far-away country that he loved—one man whom he wanted to reach; and so Black Storm held on toward the east. He traveled until near sundown and came to a wide patch of buffalo grass, bare of snow. Here he fed until nearly dark and again headed eastward.

Whether Black Storm sensed the coming of spring or not cannot be known, for no man can completely enter the mind of a horse to understand. It may be that the Maker who made man and horses did let him understand, and it must have been at least that the starving Black Storm did have hope, like the hope that stirs in men with the nearness of spring. At any rate being driven from the feeding ground that had sustained him, he moved steadily toward the east and now and then a little south of east. He may not have had the sure instinct telling him how to travel by the nearest route home, still he was moving for the most part in that general direction.

On and on he moved across that vast country of plains with its never-ending stretch of wintry wastes, the distant, long, cheerless ridges with their patches of snow and cold, gray rocks; and always the gloomy skyline that hovered in the distance above them.

Black Storm knew that at one time, far beyond those bleak, wintry ridges, there had been a world of sunshine, the green grasses of summer and more than all beside—the man. Also in that far-away land there had been little human beings that made loud noises, but who never hurt, and who also at times had brought the sugar-food and the kindly hands.

And now all that Black Storm knew was this: he was moving toward this land, the land of Joe Bain. Probably he did not even think how he would find food but he did know how to hunt for the buffalo grass where the snow had not covered the ground and he knew also that the tender twigs of the cottonwoods that grew along the streams were good for him. He did not know that he was hundreds of miles from the man he loved—but he did know in a vague way that it was a long, long way, a very long way and that he was always in danger.

As he traveled on, the gloom of the winter night came down, and there came the steady crunching sounds of his hoofs as they ground into the surface of the frozen snow.

## Chapter XIV

### TRAGEDY

*O*LD Round Top, on a high hill range of the West, stands serene, majestic, keeping eternal watch through winter and summer over the two river valleys below. The generations have come and gone but Old Round Top, silent, sober, unchanged, has witnessed the drama of men and horses.

And again this ancient hill looked down on the droning and throbbing of life, for spring had come and passed into early June. The day

was still and warm. Golden flowers of the shoot-
ing-star were blooming on the valley; mist-like
blooms of the meadow-rue stood as if looking
and listening toward the hilltop, and the whole
valley lay hushed and still as though in waiting
for him who now appeared on the top of the
hill—a beautiful, black horse. He stood looking,
anxious and lonely, still longing, hoping,
searching for one man, and likewise always fearing the approach of those who would hurt him.

Here Black Storm had reached a rough
country of high bluffs and deep ravines. After
standing for some time on the high summit of
Old Round Top, he started down a narrow
trail on the hillside, picking his way carefully
among the rough stones until he was nearly to
the level below. Here he turned south and
rounded the base of another stony bluff to find
directly in his path a long narrow cut, some six
feet deep and four feet wide. Black Storm did
here what he had done many times before at
these narrow steep cuts—leaped across. He
easily cleared the cut but as his feet struck on
the other side, a pain shot through the frog
of his right front foot—a pain like a knife-
thrust. He groaned and stood for a little holding the foot up and when he tried to go on he
could not touch the foot to the ground. One of
those peculiar tragedies that happened at times
to his kind in the West had come to Black

Storm. There were pieces of flint here as hard
and as sharp as steel and when Black Storm
leaped the cut, he had alighted on one of these
upturned arrow-like fragments which had bur-
ied itself in the soft part of his foot. The pain
was incessant and excruciating, and Black
Storm was as helpless as a small child. He did
not know how to relieve himself—only knew
that he felt the knife-like pain and that he could
not stand it to put the foot to the ground.

In this helpless situation he became fearful
that his human enemies might discover him,
and hard and painful as it was, he started toward a little woods standing on some level
ground about a quarter of a mile away. Slowly
he moved on three legs, lurching himself forward, in the hard, awkward manner a horse
must do when he can go only on three legs.

When half way toward the small wood he
came to another low ditch which crossed his
path. Black Storm stood helpless before this,
quivering and trembling with pain. Then
slowly with a lunge of his body he started along
the edge of the ditch to find a crossing. There
seemed to be no end to the cut although he
hobbled on for a long distance. Then on reaching a place that looked to him as if he might
cross, he stopped. At the same time he looked
anxiously behind him for he heard a suspicious
sound far to the south in the wooded hills.

Afraid that he heard men, he lurched down into the ditch, stumbled and fell hard, his head striking against a bowlder. In falling, he instinctively threw out both front feet to catch himself and a violent pain shot through both his head and his foot. He lay for a moment on his side, while dark and yellow spots danced in his eyes. When his vision cleared he struggled to his feet and on across the plain toward the woods with its friendly thickets and spreading elm trees.

On reaching the shelter Black Storm limped in until he was well within the cover of the trees, then stopped, and cocking his ears up, listened. He could hear no sounds that suggested the men, and after a time he drew a long sigh and began moving his forefoot, trying to ease the steady throbbing; now and then giving a start when an unusually sharp pain shot through the foot.

The sun outside the shady grove was shining brightly on a peaceful world. Black Storm, feeling weak and ill, slowly lay down on the ground under a great silent spreading tree. He closed his eyes and tried to sleep. Little splashes of sunlight filtered through the leafy tree and fell on his beautiful black coat. At last he laid his head down on the cool, damp earth of the woods. For a time he felt the pain in his foot, but at last some good angel seemed to help him,

and he slowly drifted off into unconsciousness;
for the time he knew no fear, no pain, no heart-
breaking run, no hunger, no thirst—and all was
still in the little grove. Once a bluejay alighted
on a bough above, but even he with his petu-
lant disposition only looked down for a moment, then silently flew away. A chipmunk sat
up, looking from his hole under a root—looking but making no sound. Two red squirrels,
that had been crossly scolding a short time before, seemed to find no fault here and now lay
in their nests, their heads outside in the sun,
looking down on him who lay so still below. A
redbird who had just sung his joy in the river
woods, suddenly came out of the blue to alight
on a bough of the spreading elm, but he, too,
only looked down quietly, and as if he knew he
should not break the silence here, flew softly
away.

Black Storm lay with his wounded foot bent
up toward his body, his vast black tail spread
down on the ground as if human hands had
carefully arranged it there. His long, heavy
mane had fallen back and lay in a mass, partly
on his neck and partly on the clear earth behind him. He did not sleep well for long, and
after a time, as he tried to doze, he would flinch
and jerk his wounded foot quickly, then as the
pain eased a little he would again close his eyes.
But at last he could no longer rest for the pain

began stabbing him constantly. He had to get
to his feet and here was a hard thing, for, to do
this, he had to get up on his front feet first. He
began the struggle, throwing his weight on the
one front foot while trying to protect the in-
jured one. With the well foot out in front of
him he tried to lunge upward, failed the first
time, but the second time, he struggled up. In
the effort the other foot, which he had always
used so naturally, struck the ground and he
stood in silence holding the foot up while he
endured the pain.

Presently he limped to the edge of the trees
and looked anxiously out. There were no
sounds nor signs of men, and being thirsty, he
moved out slowly along the open, keeping in
the smooth path of a cattle trail that seemed to
invite him straight across the level valley. As
Black Storm walked slowly forward, the trail
grew wider and wider and on either side smaller
cattle trails led into it. He knew by instinct, as
every horse that ran along on the range knew,
that when the cattle trail thus stretches away
becoming steadily wider, it always leads to
water.

Black Storm moved on for a long distance,
stopping time after time to rest and look and
listen—and then at last he saw not far beyond
a wide, shallow stream with a small fringe of
willows along its margin and with many deep-

cut cattle trails leading down its high sandy
bank to the shining water. He moved up until
he came to one of the steep trails leading down
through the bank. Here he looked longingly at
the water, but still hesitated. In his condition,
to move downward was most difficult of all. At
last he started down, thumping his way by hard,
heaving jerks on one front leg until he reached
the sandy margin of the clear, shallow river. He
drank long and feverishly, then raised his head
to look out across the stream. Many long sand
bars stretched out in the water, far up and down
the river, and here and there, around the margin of small shallow pools, killdeer were moving and catching minnows, the while shrilling
their clear piping notes to one another across
the bars. Black Storm stood for a long time
looking. Then some instinct telling him if he
would cross the river he could get farther away
from his enemies and nearer home, he started
out, carefully picking his way over the firm,
dry sand of the bars; but now and then he came
to swift little shallows that he was compelled to
cross and as often as he did this, painful though
it was, he stood on his well foot and put the
wounded one in the water to test the firmness
of the bottom, for Black Storm had learned long
since the meaning of quicksand in rivers. Many
times during his days with Joe Bain, Joe had discovered this and when riding across the shallow

Republican River, Joe learned that when Black Storm stopped or backed away, that he had somehow sensed the treacherous quicksand. At such times Joe had given him his head, and then picking his way, Black Storm would get safely across on firm sand. He was doing this now only he was more afraid because he had only three legs to help him. With all his legs well he would have boldly pushed out in the stream and found his way around the patches of quicksand within a few minutes, but now he was almost an hour—putting his nose down often, to sniff a suspicious place; at the same time feeling it a little with his wounded foot, then lurching himself around the treacherous spot, and smelling and testing again, until at last he reached the low, shelving bank on the opposite side.

Limping out a short distance on the dry, soft sand he got slowly down and lay on his side, but he kept his head up and looked back across the wide river. Would his enemies appear there at any moment? This thought was in his brain and it made him miserable. As the time slipped by, however, there was no sign of men. The flies began biting him and he threw his head back time after time to drive them away from his shoulder. Then Nature helped him. A friendly cowbird alighted near him on the sand, and then boldly flew up on Black Storm's side and began picking off the sticking flies. Moving from place to place on the great body of the horse the cowbird continued to snap up the insects. Black Storm accepted the natural comfort and paid no heed to the bird but he still looked anxiously across the river.

At the end of an hour the misery in his foot compelled him to get to his feet. Slowly he passed up the sloping sand to the grassland beyond.

Not far down the stream, there grew on this side a long fringe of tall, green willows, stretching far away into the east where they followed a wide bend in the river, and growing all along the valley there was a rank growth of luxurious green grass.

Black Storm made his way to this place and when near the willows he began with difficulty to reach down to crop off the grass. Every now and then, while munching a mouthful, he raised his head to look about him.

Within a small circle here of not many rods across, he passed the day. A number of times he lay down, but never long for his foot gave him no peace.

Night fell, and he was still close to the willows. With the coming of darkness Black Storm started out on the valley toward the east; he held on in this direction as straight as possible, but time after time was compelled to go out of his course to pass around steep sand-hills and winding ravines.

Morning found him completely exhausted in a small clump of trees. He dropped down to the earth here and for a time was almost asleep when all of a sudden he was startled by voices. Instantly he raised his head but did not try to get up when he saw two small boys walking near the grove. The boys were sons of John Marston, one of the few ranchmen in this region. Suddenly one of the boys stopped and exclaimed, "Oh, look! There's a pretty black horse!"

They came up rather timidly but when Black Storm only lay still and looked wonderingly at them, they came closer and finally put their hands on him. Black Storm made low sounds of trust and friendliness.

"Oh, look there!" said one of the boys, "one of his feet is terribly swollen! He's hurt, I wish Father was at home!"

They both stood looking with deep concern at Black Storm's foot. Both the foot and leg were now swollen, the latter up beyond the knee. A sudden impulse seized them, and the boys ran pell mell to the house to tell their mother. With more work than she could do, she nevertheless went back with them the while listening to their excited voices.

Black Storm whinnied a little as the woman came up and he was not afraid. Mrs. Marston looked at the swollen foot and then got as close as she dared and looked again. "You poor thing," she said. "He's got something in his foot but we can do nothing until your father and the men come home, but we can bring him water and feed. You poor thing!" she repeated, patting Black Storm gently on his head, and then after looking at him for a little she went back to the house.

The two boys ran on ahead of her and getting some buckets, they carried water and grain to Black Storm. He ate and drank without getting up and showed his appreciation of their kindness by low whinnying. The boys put their hands on his head and talked to him. They both looked very seriously at his foot; and one of them, taking some cold water that was left in a pail, walked up and gently poured it on the swelling. This felt soothing to the foot and Black Storm did not move, only flinched a little when the cold water first touched the sore.

All that afternoon the boys carried cold water, and after giving Black Storm all he would drink, they poured what was left in the bucket on his wounded foot, and remained by him and comforted him until the night came and they had to go to the house.

An hour passed, and another, and still another, and none of the men had come home. They were unusually late on this night. Then came the sounds of many hoofbeats on the prairie and Black Storm raised his head, suddenly alert.

John Marston and a dozen of his cowboys came riding past the grove. Black Storm could hear the rattle and jangle of the wheels and bells on the spurs as the men jogged along. He trembled like a leaf for he was helpless and he knew it. In his nervous fear he wanted to get up and try to battle against them, for it seemed to him they would come in the grove and take him, and that he must go through all the old suffering again. But he lay still, with his head up, watching.

Marston and his cowboys rode on, without a suspicion of what was lying in the clump of trees.

An hour later, John Marston, by direction of his wife, took a lantern and a pair of pincers, and walked out to the grove. He was soon among the trees, supposing he would at once see a large black horse lying there with a wounded front foot. He hunted about for a time, holding the lantern up to get a better view in the darkness. To his surprise he saw no horse. He then not only looked carefully in the small grove but walked out some distance and made a complete circle around the place, searching the open at every point. It was no use—Black Storm had gone.

## Chapter XV

### DUST AND HAIL

IT was late one afternoon some days later. Black Storm was hobbling along with his badly swollen foot, headed toward the southwest. He passed with great difficulty through a trough in some sand-hills and stopped on the higher ground to rest. Here, perhaps for the space of fifteen minutes, he stood, trying to ease himself, when he suddenly forgot his misery and looked about him with apprehension. Although he did not understand it, it seemed to him that things around him did not look as they should. There was a reddish tinge in the air, and the sun, that had been brightly shining, had become dim and almost hidden in a strange darkened veil. The wind that blew almost constantly across the plains had ceased. Ground birds that had been flitting about over the prairie a short time before had now vanished, and not even a rabbit nor a prairie dog could be seen.

It all seemed so strange to Black Storm and somehow instinct warned him that there was danger. He had been facing the southwest, but now he lurched around and looked back. Instantly he was alarmed. He saw, coming down from the north, a vast, swiftly moving, reddish-looking cloud—a cloud as far on either side as the eye could see—one of the worst dust storms in the history of Western Kansas was bearing down upon him.

He turned and started limping down a long incline, knowing he should be in shelter, but not knowing where to find it.

Before he had gone a dozen rods the dust storm struck him. Instinctively he shut his eyes and at the same time coughed, for in that instant the dust was in his nostrils, his throat, and he even felt the sting of it in his closed eyes.

Although the late evening sun had been still faintly shining through a veil, the day now suddenly went almost dark and there was a wild, incessant roaring about his ears. Like a thing alive it seized him, whipped him, jerked him, hissed and howled, the while driving sand and grit in his mouth, his nose, his eyes, his ears, and at times beating him so violently he was almost knocked from his feet. For a time he was completely bewildered. Blinking his eyes, coughing and half choking, weaving and battling to keep his feet, he heaved forward, going with the whirling, rushing wind and dust.

If it had not been for his wounded foot, Black Storm would have run with the seething storm and in all probability would have found a low ravine or a wood along a stream that would have given him some shelter. But as it was, he had to struggle hard to keep on his feet, and once, moving blindly along, he missed his footing by stepping on a round stone just as a violent surge of wind struck him. He fell heavily. For a moment everything seemed to be swimming about him. He lay, holding his head as high as he could, shutting his eyes tight to try to relieve them of the stinging from the driving sand.

If Black Storm had now given up and remained here, he likely would have met death in what was to follow. But his was a spirit not of the average. If he died, he would die fighting.

After recovering himself a little he struggled to his feet—struggled and fell three times—his eyes still closed, pain shooting through them; stabbing pains running through his foot while the blinding storm still howled around him. Again he tried and this time got on his three well legs. Then again he started forward—he knew not where, only he must battle to get out of all this.

On he plodded, and on, until a quivering weakness ran through him. And now he heard, above the roar of the blinding dust, another sound, a roar that sounded steady, sinister, louder than the roar of the dust storm; steadily louder it came and nearer and nearer, and then the dust storm vanished in a deafening, blinding crash of ten million hailstones beating on the earth, and the night fell black around him.

In this moment of darkness and confusion, Black Storm felt the ground caving down under his front foot. Violently he tried to recover himself only to pitch down with the caving earth into a shallow creek-bed ten feet below. He fell with his head and half of his body in a tangled thicket of wild grapevines and small trees. The branches of some low cottonwoods, through which he crashed when he fell, closed together after his body passed through them. These boughs and the vines of the thickets broke the worst of the hail from him, and he did not try to get up. Putting his head close to the earth he took what shelter he could while hailstones, some as large as a hen's egg, beat furiously down with an incessant, deafening roar. Now and then one pelted through the thicket to strike him and send a sharp pain through the rear part of his body; once an immense hailstone crashed clear through the twigs and vines and

struck him on the head. For an instant he was
dazed by the blow and dark spots danced before his eyes, but his vision cleared and his
shelter still saved him.

For an hour the hail roared and pelted down,
then began to lessen and a cold rain began driving down, moaning and howling through the
trees and thickets along the little stream. With
this, Black Storm raised his head a little. The
drenching water made him bat his eyes, but it
also washed the sand and grit from them and
eased the smarting.

Black Storm's shelter was poor, but better
than none, and something in his brain told him
that miserable as he was he should remain here.
Hour after hour he lay in the thicket and endured the misery, often shaking his head and
snorting when the thing seemed almost unbear-
able.

While the hail for the most part had ceased
there was still now and then a loud crash and
thump near him, that warned him that another
fearful blow on the head might come if he
moved away from the vines. Miserable as he
was he at last fell into a brief dreaming sleep—
sometimes lifting his head, fully conscious, and
again letting it sink down in a half-stupor with
the storm roaring over the vines and trees.

The hours dragged by, and at last morning
came—came with a clear sky and a drenched,

hushed world. Again Black Storm was on his feet. He heaved his way through the thin belt of timber along the stream and came out in view of the land beyond—a land silent, lonely, dreary, frowning, awaiting him who now ventured upon it.

Far away in that uncertain distance, toward which Black Storm looked in his pain and longing, was a stranger, a human being yet a friend, if only chance, or the good angel of all four-footed things who suffer, might guide the horse to him. Yet Black Storm knew not and he started uncertainly across the lonely plain.

All that day and the next he struggled on. He stopped now and then to graze on the buffalo grass or drink at some little hillside spring; but as the days and nights passed he ate less and less and drank more and more water, for a fever had laid hold of him. And now as he moved on, dragging his swollen leg, he was so sick he lost all fear and all caution. He was too weak to care now—the end was not far away—and nothing mattered—only one last, heart-breaking longing came to him. Vaguely, blindly, yet like the instinct of a child, it was in his brain, that if he could get to the one man in the world, *he* would help. But chance is a singular thing. Black Storm still fought on, the while unconsciously moving toward a human friend, yet that friend was not Joe Bain.

## Chapter XVI

### TOM AND RACHEL STANLEY

*I*N a remote spot of Kansas, in a region of beautiful valleys and uplands, many miles southwest of the Kaw River, young Tom Stanley lived on a farm with his wife, Rachel, and small son, James. Far to the west and still farther southwest of them, was the great cattle country, but Tom and Rachel knew little of this, for theirs was only a small farm near which the great herds of longhorn cattle sometimes passed.

Early September had come. The upland plovers were calling in the early morning on the pastures; sunflowers were spreading their yellow mantles on valley and hill under the brooding autumnal haze. Goldenrod and purple asters stood in the hush along low bluff-sides and winding, deep-cut cattle trails.

One still morning just at sunrise Tom Stanley was moving out toward his corral when he saw in the distance something that arrested his attention. Moving across the high prairie from the west was what was left of a once beautiful black horse. Tom saw him struggling along on three legs, painfully dragging a front one. The young man hurried out to meet him as the horse came slowly on. When Rachel came out in the yard she saw her husband and the horse behind the corral. Tom shouted, "Oh! Rachel! bring me the pinchers and come look at this horse's foot!"

Wondering, she hurried into the tool house, then came running out behind the corral, James, their six-year-old child, following her.

"Oh! his poor foot!" she said, shuddering as she handed Tom the pinchers.

"It's the worst I ever saw," said he. "There's a piece of flint in his foot—I can see it—if he'll only hold still."

Tom held the swollen foot and leg up gently, and as gently applied the pinchers. Black Storm groaned and flinched when Tom with a twist and a jerk brought the thing out. Instantly the poison began running from the wound.

"It's been weeks in there to cause all this," said Tom. "Just see his condition."

Black Storm stood with his weight on three legs, wasted and thin, because for weeks he had been so sick he had scarcely eaten the green grass that grew around him.

"We'll get the poor thing in the barn and put hot vinegar poultices on his foot," said Rachel as she hurried to the house while Tom moved slowly with Black Storm to the stable.

For the first week Black Storm drank feverishly of the water they brought to him but he would eat very little. James was permitted to bring him lumps of sugar and these Black Storm ate. With the beginning of the second week his appetite came and the swelling in his foot was rapidly going down. When three weeks had passed he was taking on flesh rapidly and he now put the wounded foot on the ground, though he still walked with a limp. Finally, as the days went by he walked as of old and his beauty increased each day. If Tom and Rachel Stanley had not seen the transformation, they could not have believed it. They admired him, petted him and wondered about him, and always they noticed that he seemed restless, as if looking and expecting something or somebody.

It was during this time that Black Storm developed a peculiar attachment for the child, James. This must have been partly due, at least, to the fact that James many times each day came into the house, saying, "I want some more brown sugar for that big, black horse." At least half of the time he was given a lump and carried it out to Black Storm.

James had a small sand pile north of the house where he played alone through the long autumn hours and sometimes the sun shone very warm there. On several occasions Rachel Stanley found him playing in his sand pile with Black Storm standing near by. Once, late on a warm afternoon, Rachel finished some of her work, and thinking of James, hurried out to see where he was. At first she was a little frightened. She saw Black Storm lying down; James lay asleep beside his sand pile, his curly blonde hair against the great black mane of Black Storm. Black Storm, also, was asleep, his nose almost touching the ground, his eyes closed.

Slowly Rachel approached, fearing she might frighten Black Storm and cause him to spring up suddenly. But when she got as far as the little sand pile all fear left her. Black Storm opened his sleepy eyes a little, saw who it was, and again closed them and slept, perhaps dreaming of all he longed for.

Rachel stood for a moment, disliking to take James away. The child slept with his face upturned, one knee bent a little, a bare foot resting on the prairie sod and another in the sand.

A half-dozen little crude cornstalk horses that he had whittled out lay about on the sand, and one of them lay in the open palm of his hand which rested against the great shoulder of Black Storm.

It was plain that Black Storm had chosen this place to lie down and that James, in the spirit of adventure, had laid his head in the soft mane. With such a soft pillow and the warm sun, nature had carried him away in sleep.

Rachel went up quietly and lifted James up. He protested when he was fully awake, and was pacified only by being told he might bring out another lump of sugar for Black Storm.

The autumn days were now moving swiftly by. A sober haze hung listless over hills and valley, and the last of the summer flowers were fading and drying on hill and plain. The sweet everlastings with their once beautiful pearly flowers now hung withered and lifeless on the pensive landscape. And as if to bring a last kindly greeting to a passing friend, the golden aster stood living and blooming in the solemn hush of the valley.

Far beyond the Stanley home, where in these days Black Storm sometimes stood and looked afar, lay a wide and shining river with a dying fringe of willows far up and down its waters. And sometimes as Black Storm stood and looked at the river, shining in the autumn sun, a faint breeze carried to his nostrils the odor of the water and the sands and the willows, and it was the same as it was when he had been on the Republican River—where he had lived with Joe Bain. And so now, day after day, Black Storm would stand on the highest hill and look toward the east and the distant river; and each day he seemed to grow more and more restless.

On every side of him as far as he could see were the distant, haze-covered hills, and the vast plains with their gray withered grass, the silent, listless, lone trees dotting the landscape and always the river with its long borders of silent trees; the river seemed always calling him to a land his heart so much wanted. He did not know the direction, but each day he grew more and more miserable; something was tugging at his heart and calling—calling to the land of Joe Bain.

They now no longer tied him but gave him the freedom of the place, yet he did not leave the yard except to graze a little beyond the corral, and was always ready for his feed at night. Many times they saw him standing with his head high, his ears pricked forward, looking toward the east, and a number of times they heard him neigh loudly.

One evening as they stood watching him do this Tom said, "I can't figure out what it is he wants. It's not the other horses for I have brought them to him and they do not seem to do him any good. Last night I put him in the corral with them to see if he could be satisfied, but he wasn't and for a long time he stood there, paying no attention to them, but holding his head up and looking out toward the east neighing. He wants something or somebody but I don't know what it is."

"It may be he wants some man who owned him—some man he has become attached to," said Rachel. "You know there is a horse now and then who will do that."

"That's so," said Tom thoughtfully. "It might be that, and I guess we had better begin tying him up and see if someone is hunting him. He's getting so restless now I'm afraid he'll go away. We can go to the nearest newspaper and advertise him, and if no one ever calls, we can then honestly keep him."

As they sat in the house that night talking of him, they heard a loud shrill neigh out near the stables.

"There he is again," said Tom, "his mind is more and more lonesome for somebody or something."

"Did you tie him tonight?" asked Rachel.

"No," Tom said, "he's in the corral with the other horses. I put all the bars up at the gate, he's never tried to jump out."

For two hours that night at intervals of every

few minutes, Black Storm neighed, and once Tom and Rachel went out to talk to him and quiet him. He looked at them as they stood near the gate of the corral and put his nose up to each of them when they held their hands out to him, but this time even with the two present, he would raise his head, look toward the north and east and neigh shrilly. At last they gave it up and went in the house for the night.

The next morning when Tom went to the corral he found all the horses there except Black Storm. The top pole of the high gate was knocked down on one end and a study of the ground outside revealed the tracks of a horse leading eastward. Tom carefully followed the trail down to a little spring in a bluff side. Here Black Storm had apparently stopped to drink for two large fresh hoofprints were in the wet earth close to the spring.

Tom came back, a look of disappointment on his face.

"He's leaped the corral and gone, Rachel," he said. "I'm going to get on a horse and hunt him."

It was late afternoon when Tom came back, put up his horse and came wearily in the house.

"No use, Rachel," he said—"not a sign of him. It may be as you say—it may be it's some man he wants and is trying to get to him. I don't know who it is, but I hope he finds him."

## Chapter XVII

### TRAPPED WITH THE WILD HORSES

**W**HEN Black Storm left Tom and Rachel Stanley he did not do so because he did not feel their great kindness to him. He did feel it and although they were not aware of it, they had been very unusual people in his life of trouble. But to Black Storm there was but one human being who had completely won him and that was Joe Bain.

It may be well here to observe that the attachment of this unusual horse for Joe Bain can be explained in only one way. The dramatic manner in which they first met does not explain it all for that was only the beginning. It can be explained only by saying that Joe Bain understood horses as few men understood them, and with all of his understanding of them, he was always the same, steady, calm, quiet youth who was never ruffled, who was always thoughtful of them, and always kind. Black Storm then got this on his brain and he could not forget.

It is true that Helen McDonald had lavished kindness upon the horse and there was never any question but that he trusted her fully, for she could mount him at will and ride him whither she would—a thing he had never permitted anyone to do but Joe Bain. For even when the McDonald men had later mounted him without spurs he instantly threw them, for he could never get over his fear of any man mounting him except Bain. Yet, if the McDonald men did not actually try to mount him, he did not seem to fear them and he allowed them to be around him and handle him in any way they chose. So, again, it must have been that this youthful cattle foreman of the old West somehow communicated his love in a peculiar manner to Black Storm. At any rate there is no question but that in all of Black Storm's wandering and his misery, he did not forget the tall, slim, dark youth; and it must have been that when he left Tom and Rachel Stanley he did so still longing in his own way to find Joe Bain. As for Joe Bain, although he had owned many horses, he had never had one to which he became attached as he had to this one; and likewise, he had never met with a disappointment so bitter as when he lost him. It is also of record that he never ceased to hunt for him.

On this day, as Black Storm traveled across the plains, in a sense moving vaguely and blindly, the chance of ever seeing Joe Bain might have seemed slight indeed, for he was traveling now not toward the McDonald ranch, but fully two hundred miles south and west of it. Being fully well, as he was, and traveling in a country where there were small streams where he might drink as often as he liked, and finding the luxurious growth of buffalo grass that had now withered, but cured on the ground, he had all he wished to sustain him, yet he was lonely—always lonely. And once again he would have been glad to see some of his own kind—not that he would have remained long with them, for thus far he had not done so although he had been given the opportunity—but a temporary meeting with them in some way was to his desire.

When Tom Stanley had come up to him that

morning, Black Storm had been too sick and too near death to fear any man. But now in good flesh again and wholly himself, his old fear of men returned and he was no sooner out of sight of the Stanley home than he began to be alert, suspicious and watchful.

It was about noon of his second day out that he saw danger. He had been moving at an easy pace, stopping now and then to look searchingly across all the land about him, when, on coming to the top of a high ridge, he saw in a valley not far below him, a dozen or more horsemen riding leisurely along, some of them behind, and a number in front, of a long string of Texas Longhorn cattle. Black Storm gave one quick look, then quickly whirled, trotted back down the hill to the level, and broke into a run, keeping at the foot of the bluff until it ended near a low rocky canyon that led southwest. He galloped into the canyon, stopped and looked back, his head and tail raised, and with a snort of fear he turned and started at a rapid trot along the depths of the canyon, his hoofs resounding with a sharp clatter on the gray rocky bottom.

For two miles he kept up the pace and then on reaching a point where the ground above dipped down in a sharp, but passable, incline, he leaped up the shelving ground and galloped away over the plain, throwing his head from side to side and looking behind him as he ran.

Seeing no more signs of his enemies he finally slowed down and traveled at a more leisurely pace until night.

Then one of the strangest and most dramatic experiences of his stormy life came to him. He was still traveling at a walk when in the almost black darkness he passed down a slope of ground to see just ahead of him, all standing huddled together, a considerable herd of wild horses. Although Black Storm never knew, it happened, nevertheless, that when he was still a quarter of a mile from this herd, human eyes saw him pass in—for two men on that side, standing near their mounts and holding their horses' noses so the animals could not whinny, saw him and gladly let him walk into the trap —for trap it proved to be.

For more than a week fully thirty of some of the most skillful cowboys and ropers of the old West had ridden and so skillfully maneuvered that they had at last got the wild mustangs surrounded, a feat that was seldom indeed accomplished even by the most patient and skillful of horsemen.

The stallion who led the wild horses snorted loudly when Black Storm approached, and frightened and angry, came out to meet him, ears laid back, deadly teeth bared. Black Storm halted, looked at the dark shape coming toward him, heard the angry squeal of the stallion that told him the horse meant danger—then as the stallion reached to slash him, Black Storm leaped aside, and like the strike of a snake he drove both of his mighty hoofs against the side of the wild leader. One hoof struck the shoulder and the smaller horse was knocked to his knees; before he could recover Black Storm again drove his heels against him. With a snort the stallion, angered at the power of this newcomer, shrank back and stood close to the herd facing Black Storm. But Black Storm was not looking for battle; he only wanted to defend himself. He walked respectfully around to the other side of the herd, and after seeing that they were all unfriendly and suspicious of him, he stood a little off. With a low whinny he told them he only wanted companionship, then made the best of things by trying to be content that they would even let him stand near them. He saw that they scarcely stood still a moment, but kept moving a little as they huddled together, and there was no sign that they would quiet down, closing their eyes to rest and doze in the night, as he wished to do.

For some time Black Storm stood looking at them. Not understanding their actions but growing somewhat accustomed to them, he let his head fall and dozed fitfully for a considerable time. But every now and then he was somewhat startled by the unusual crowding and jostling of the wild horses. At last, they made him uneasy; it seemed to him that something was wrong yet he did not know what; he grew apprehensive and tried to peer out in the darkness, but the night was so black he could see nothing.

A little to the west of the level ground where the wild horses stood was a long high ledge of rock, and not far to the south of this flowed a small, sluggish stream which wound its way through a long, very narrow, steep, rocky canyon. This was the only outlet to the place, an almost circular hill looming high and frowning on all sides.

At last Black Storm grew so apprehensive he could no longer remain with the wild horses. He started out slowly, trying to find a way out. At first he moved up to the rocky wall on the west, then turned and walked along the base of the ledge until he came to the sloping ground. He paused here a minute, then started up. When less than halfway up he whirled back with a frightened snort. A man standing above him had lighted a match.

Slowly Black Storm circled the base of the circular hill and at last came upon the small stream leading out through the narrow canyon. This seemed the way out although he did not know that the wild stallion had already tried it.

Black Storm walked on the sod beside the

stream for a little distance, then stepped down on the flat rocks bordering the water. Here he stopped and looked a long time ahead of him. The stars shone down on the narrow stream and shadowy ledges. A small lone cedar stood a little below, and some bushes loomed dark and hushed beyond the lone tree. All was complete silence, yet Black Storm was suspicious. A scent came to his nostrils that warned him, yet he could see no sign of life. He moved slightly on the flat rocks and was startled by a splash in the water as a stone fell from the ledge on the other side. Again he paused, looking, fearing treachery. He could hear plainly the crowding of the wild horses and the thumping as their hoofs beat upon the sod behind him.

After several minutes Black Storm started forward again. He passed the lone cedar and was approaching the bushes when suddenly two men leaped out in front of him shaking buffalo robes. Terror-stricken he whirled and ran like a streak back up the canyon and again got close to his companions in danger. He could no longer rest now for he was as nervous and fearful as they. He kept up a constant movement, working around them, stopping and looking, now toward the high circular bluff, and now toward the narrow canyon where he had been so frightened; and then again he would stop and look out in the night.

## Chapter XVIII

### THE OLD, OLD ENEMY

*A*LL through the hours of the night Black Storm stood near the wild horses and looked in wonder and apprehension at their restlessness. The wild stallion at least was not quiet for a moment. With his ears cocked stiffly forward he looked out into the vague darkness and uttered loud snorts, telling plainly that he was fearful of something. Once or twice he pranced around the herd; each time, as he did so, he paid little heed to Black Storm, who stood quietly a little away from the others. Finally, Black Storm also grew restless and an instinctive fear of men-enemies came to him. With this, he walked out a little farther from the jostling, nervous herd; and once he passed clear around them. Then to his nostrils came a suspicious scent and at the same time he heard the loud sound made by a horse some distance beyond, blowing through his nostrils.

Black Storm now became as nervous and as frightened as the wild horses and all of a sudden there surged in him a strong feeling of companionship for them. He trotted back to the herd and in the darkness came up so close to the small wild stallion that he touched him, but neither of them now seemed troubled with the presence of the other, and both stood side by side looking toward the higher ground and snorting with fear at the peril. Each sensed fully they were in a trap—a common enemy had surrounded them.

As the darkness slowly faded and the gray dawn lighted the near-by crests around them, Black Storm started with the others running wildly in a small circle, but look as they would for an opening, there was none—the circular ridge around them was alive with mounted men. Twice the daring stallion started out, but in the face of booming six-shooters, he was turned, and terrified, ran back. And now the early light of day was upon them.

At this moment the men with wild yells came riding down upon the herd, swinging their lariats and all driving toward the frightened horses in the center. On the instant Black Storm whirled to run toward a narrow gap between the oncoming riders, but at the same moment the entire herd of panic-stricken horses rushed upon him and he struck into their midst so hard the breath was nearly knocked out of him. He was completely checked in his rush, and oddly enough the wild stallion was also caught in the jam. For a little they bore Black Storm back and held him like a vise. He struggled up with all his powerful muscles, and with his head and upper body above the mass struck out madly, his forehoofs striking the backs of the mustangs. The stallion had half-turned and also reared to his hind legs, struggling to get free of the frenzied plunging mass. The riders were rushing in from every direction. A dense cloud of dust was kicked up and hovered over the squealing, surging horses. Black Storm was nearly out when through the dust a whirl-noose settled over his high head; and almost simultaneously the stallion was also caught with one of the hissing ropes. Black Storm felt a sudden terrific jerk on his throat and he fell with the hoofs of a dozen mustangs crashing over him.

Half-dazed he tried to struggle up, and did so with wild horses running in every direction, while hard-riding, yelling men, pursued them. The dust from the little plain cleared and Black Storm stood on his feet, shaking like an aspen leaf, a rope now holding him from either side. Not far away from him the wild stallion was battling futilely against his captors.

Unfortunately, it was a group of very thoughtless men who had surrounded the wild horses and Black Storm. And a hard fate awaited the beautiful stallion. With more than necessary cruelty he was roped, thrown and tied, the saddle fastened upon him and the ropes on his front feet cut loose. But while they held him with the long ropes, and before a man could mount him, he leaped to his feet, reared high in the air, lost his balance and fell backward; the back of his head struck with fearful impact against a flat stony surface behind him. He grew limp, unconscious, and lay still. The men, rough as they were, looked serious. They had not expected that this would happen.

They now turned to Black Storm and to their great surprise found he was easily saddled. But now, even though two men held him with long ropes, he threw each of them in turn as they mounted and the last man fell hard.

At this moment there came a hearty laugh behind them and the three turned to see a short, dark man whom none of them knew.

"He's just that much black dynamite, boys—I've seen pitching horses, but never one like him. Say now!" the stranger broke off suddenly, "he'll never be any good to you—suppose you take a hundred dollar bill and I take the horse."

The men could scarcely credit their good fortune, for in these days, a hundred dollars was much money to a cowboy. They handed over the rope that held Black Storm, took the one hundred dollar bill and rode away.

When they had gone, the man walked slowly up to Black Storm, patted him a little and said, "I see you are dynamite to ride, and I'm going to take you where plenty of men can try you—but that's all they can try. You're a beauty anyway, I take it, and you're no mustang—you're just a tame horse, but an outlaw—well now! You lead real nice-like," the man continued, as Black Storm instantly followed him. "Queer you pitch so awful." Then fixing the rope so it acted as a halter for Black Storm the man mounted his horse and rode away toward the south.

Black Storm moved along without making trouble, and when at last the night came he still followed easily enough at the pace the stranger had set, but he followed with a heavy heart.

## Chapter XIX

### JOE BAIN ARRIVES AT WICHITA

*W*HEN Joe Bain arrived in the cow town of Wichita that quiet, late autumn morning, he transacted his cattle business in less than an hour and as there would be no train for him until night, he at once set out along the streets of the town to make the same inquiry he had for many long months—had anyone seen a large, spirited black horse like Black Storm? But for the most part, Joe was a stranger in the town, meeting only now and then a big cattle buyer whom he knew and who was there on some brief business like himself.

At the end of a long search Joe was about to give up hope when, on coming to the south edge of the town, his attention was attracted to

an unusually large horse corral. There were no
horses inside the corral at the time, but as Joe
came up he noticed by the footprints in the
dust around the corral outside that there had
been many people standing and walking about
the place. He stopped and looked for a time at
the corral. It was about five feet high and well
built. A tall pole was set nearly at the top on
which hung a large American flag. The gate of
the corral opened directly out to the open
prairie and Joe walked around the place and
found that the human footprints extended well
out on this side also. He noted the prints of
the small, high-heel boots of the cowmen, also
ordinary shoe tracks and the unmistakable
prints of Indian moccasins. On the top of the
corral were large, strong poles and these were
in places worn smooth, evidently from many
persons sitting on them. Joe observed that the
corral inside showed horses' tracks. The gate
was shut. He climbed over and stood inside.
After looking at the disturbed ground he said,
"Pitching horses! Probably a free show for
everybody." Looking near one side of the corral
and apart from the other tracks, he said,
"They've got one horse that can jump," and his
keen eyes calculated the distance where the
hoofprints showed the horse had cleared a great
distance. Joe smiled, "Some cowboy went off

there and he went hard!" He bent down and
examined some of the tracks that were very
plain. "That's no broncho, that's a big horse,"
he mused. "Maybe nobody can ride him; I'll
have to find out when they have this show."

Hope was springing anew in his heart but
he did not hope too much; he had seemed to
be near his heart's desire so many times, only
to be bitterly disappointed. He walked back and
passed down the main street for some distance.
Instead of going in the many saloons he spent
his time walking about on the streets and looking at various places of amusement. As Joe
walked down the street, he now and then
greeted an acquaintance among the big cattle
men. Presently he came to Rowdy Joe's Dance
Pavilion. The scene was interesting here; he
stopped.

The dance was on. Cowboys danced with
great jangling spurs on their high-heeled boots,
mammoth sombreros on their heads. Dancing
along with these were well-dressed men in long
Prince Albert coats, cattle speculators from the
south and west. The partners of the men were
painted and jeweled women, women who for
the most part wore flaming scarlet dresses.

Around the walls of the hall-like pavilion,
and especially in the corners, were men sitting
at small tables playing poker. On some of the
tables, along with the poker chips, could be

seen little stacks of gold coins. On other tables the gold coins lay carelessly raked into a pile.

Joe stood for some time in one of the numerous doorways, then left the pavilion and turned off into a side street.

All at once he heard the doleful tunes of a hand organ. He discovered it to be just ahead of him in a very large tent. Suddenly from the inside of the tent came the loud report of a gun—this was followed by the yell of a deep voice that rose high above the sounds of the band. A man was standing up on a box near the tent announcing that tickets were for sale. Joe bought a ticket and went in. When two-thirds of the way around the tent he met, to his surprise, a short, dark man whom he knew, John Harney.

"Why, hello, Joe," Harney greeted him warmly. "Joe," he continued, "I'd rather see you than anybody. Didn't know I was running a show, did you? Well, I am and you're the very man I want and I want you bad." And a light of cunning came in Harney's dark eyes. "Say! look here, Joe," he rushed on, "you're a mighty good broncho buster, you got the reputation and I know it. Now look here; I got a horse, a big, black one that I have a show with at two o'clock every afternoon. I bought him cheap because nobody can ride him. I've made a good deal of money with him—betting that none of the cowboys can stick him. I got him from three men who had roped him while he was mixed up with some wild horses—not a man has stuck him yet. He's a fine horse, a mighty fine one, but big and throws them all like lightning. Now here's what I'll do; I'll have the show again this afternoon. The bets will be up and I'll win as I have right along, but I'm winning less and less because everybody's getting to know that horse. Now, I'll bet on you sticking on that streak of lightning and if you stay on, I'll make so much money I'll *give you the horse*. You can stick the devil if a human can do it. Come on, Joe, do you take me or not?"

The youthful, six-foot, sun-tanned Joe Bain looked with such sudden interest that he surprised Harney when he said, "Let me see him quick!" For a moment Joe stared hard into John's eyes, then he jerked out the quick, earnest words that were in his soul. Harney listened intently, then he said, "Joe, I bet I've got your horse—if I have you'll ride him anyway for me in the corral, won't you? Come on, Joe—I got all this money up—you wouldn't go back on a friend like old John Harney now, would you, Joe? You'll let them try to ride him, just this once to help *me,* seeing I got it all fixed up?"

Joe had not seemed to realize what Harney was saying but now his eyes were flashing like fire. He burst out, "Of course I'll ride that horse, but I must see him quick—I want to see if he's really my horse!"

"Come on then to the corral," said Harney, "it's time for the show right now. The boys'll have him there already. Give me a little time, Joe, give me a little time! And remember, even if he's your horse, you've promised to let the others try to ride him first!" Again Joe promised.

When they arrived at the corral a great throng of people were there and many horses of many colors, bay, brown, calico, but no great black horse among them. Joe expressed his disappointment, but Harney said, "Hold steady, he'll come—you wait a minute—you'll see in a little time now."

One at a time a number of bronchos were led in amid wild yelling and now and then the pop of a six-shooter. The cowboys rode the first horses; there were various results; some of the men were thrown, but in every case some good rider stayed on the horse and proved that he could be successfully ridden before the animal was taken out.

In the excitement of the last wildly pitching broncho, Joe did not see them lead the big black horse out—did not see him until all of a sudden the horse was led inside the corral. Instantly, pandemonium broke loose. The cowboys from sheer joy fired their six-shooters in the air, for to them, the real celebration was on at last.

Harney stood in the center of the corral holding the reins of a tall, beautiful, black gelding. The horse stood still, but twitched his ears nervously. He held his head high, a wild look of fear in his eyes, and his muscles quivered while he looked back at the man standing by the saddle.

A wild thrill shot through Joe Bain. He knew he was looking at Black Storm. He condemned himself bitterly, because he had promised that others should try to ride him.

Harney motioned for quiet and when the noise had subsided he called out in stentorian tones:

"Well!—here he is, gentlemen! As you all know he's been tried all the way from Texas to Montana and not a man has ever yet 'stuck' him. Here he is, gentlemen! Two hundred dollars to the man that can stick him! And if you all fail today I got a *tenderfoot* to ride him! Come on! Who's first today to try?"

Again pandemonium broke loose—again the wild yells and the shooting of pistols from the cowboys. One of them climbed down and the yells increased as the man approached the center of the corral. In the meantime Bain looked intently at Black Storm.

Black Storm, as of old, was not hard to ap-

proach. The first man vaulted into the saddle
and again, as on that memorable morning long
ago, a wild, black streak shot through the air;
once, twice, thrice—the man fell hard.

Another mounted. He fell as hard. Then
another and another and another. Twelve men
Black Storm threw and threw them like lightning.

Laughing good-naturedly, some of them spitting dust and blood, they set up a wild shout,
"Where's that tenderfoot? Bring him on, but
dig his grave first!"

Harney again stood in the center of the corral holding the reins of Black Storm. The horse
stood still, but twitched his ears nervously; he
still held his head high, a wild look of fear in
his eyes, and his muscles quivered while he
looked back at the man standing by the saddle.
Joe looked, his eyes flashing. He was at last
about to come up to his beloved horse! He
could scarcely wait.

Harney motioned for quiet and when the
noise had subsided he called out in stentorian
tones:

"Well, here he is still, gentlemen. As you
know, he's been tried many times and not a
man has ever yet 'stuck' him. Here he is, gentlemen. And today, I got a *tenderfoot* to ride
him, and I'm backing my tenderfoot two to
one!"

"We'll take you!" came in a chorus, and again pandemonium broke loose—again the wild yells and quick shifting from place to place among the cowboys. Joe came quickly into the corral. In that instant, there was a wild, shrill neigh and Black Storm ran to Joe, and Joe took the black head in his hands and there was a mist in the young man's eyes. Black Storm kept up a constant whinnying and it seemed he could not get close enough to Joe. The vast crowd of people suddenly grew silent in its surprise.

Still Black Storm kept up his whinnying. He rubbed his nose against Joe Bain's face, lifted a front foot as Joe had taught him to do in "shaking hands," again rubbed his face on Joe's breast, then put his head on Joe's shoulder, but quickly took it away, all the time uttering little quivering whinnyings, trying to tell from his heart how glad he was. And Joe Bain seemed to have forgotten the crowd—he could see nothing, remember nothing but Black Storm until John Harney said, "Joe, he's sure your horse and now you must ride him around the corral just to show you can do it and then you can take him away."

It had all been arranged with John Harney that if Joe could ride the horse, he was to mount him, ride him once or twice around the inside of the corral, then away without further ado. In almost complete silence Joe mounted and rode the horse once around the corral, then out at the gate and started away on the open plain.

The shouts that Joe heard behind him now made him smile.

"He ain't no tenderfoot, he can ride dynamite! He's got that horse locoed. That ain't a man on that hoss—that's a spirit! I'm gone plumb wild and crazy!"

But Joe rode on not hearing more for he could hardly credit his luck. He started out at a canter and almost constantly leaning over to pat Black Storm on the neck, he said time after time, "Seems impossible, Stormy, we found each other; we must hurry out of all this down here. I'm afraid something will happen and they'll try to get you again before I get home."

There were a number of wild cow towns on the way—towns full of evil characters and Joe planned to avoid these. Black Storm was his beautiful self again and Joe believed that the fewer men who saw him on the trail now the better. He remembered what had happened at Abilene and he was troubled. His hand went to his side to make sure his Colt's revolver was in the holster. There must be a few nights of rest on the journey, but Joe planned to take this rest in some lonely, untraveled spot where other men would not be passing.

## Chapter XX
### THE DANGEROUS TRAIL

*T*HE distance from the cow town of Wichita to the John McDonald cattle range to the northeast could be traveled on a good horse in less than a week. But Joe Bain was now making better time than most riders on this trail for he was on a horse that seemed never to tire, and one who tugged constantly on the bit to be at a brisk gallop. Black Storm did not know that if all went well he himself would be great news on the cattle range when he came galloping home—he only knew he was at peace and glad with the man he loved on his back.

Mile after mile on the wild Kansas plains, with no life to be seen save now and then a high circling hawk, a slinking coyote or a frightened rabbit, Black Storm galloped on. His mane and tail streaming in the wind, his great neck arched, his head high, his nostrils slightly distended, his luminous eyes wide and shining, he raced on toward the north.

After Joe had ridden a long distance a thing came to him that in all the joy of finding Black Storm he had forgotten. He now dismounted and looked at one of Black Storm's sides which he remembered seeing in the excitement of his pitching at Wichita. Joe uttered an exclamation of sorrow and anger when he saw that one of the horse's sides was badly wounded from the spurs. It needed attention, Joe believed, and although such things generally got well if left alone, it should nevertheless be healed as soon as possible.

A veterinary could be found in all probability in the cow town of Newton. Joe decided that he would turn aside from the trail and ride into the town to have the doctor apply medicine to both of Black Storm's sides.

It was about two hours after dark when he rode into the main street of Newton and it was less than ten minutes when he found a veterinary at a livery barn. In these days such men were hardly scientific but still they had much skill in treating wounds on horses.

The veterinary occupied a full hour in applying medicines and salves, in spite of the fact that Joe told him he wanted to get on as quickly as possible. Joe noticed that the man kept going away every now and then and saying he needed other salves or medicines and all the while he kept saying how dangerous it would be not to treat the wound fully as he saw already signs of a most dangerous sore setting in. Joe did not like the look of the man, and as he kept making such a case of the matter he began to distrust him, thinking the veterinary was trying to get as large a fee as possible.

At last the man came back after going into an alley and said that he thought Joe should not ride away at present but let the horse rest for the night. To Joe's surprise he found the fee charged was comparatively small. He paid it and began answering the questions of several men who had now come in the large stable. Joe's quick eyes noted with surprise and some apprehension that there were now fully a dozen men standing in the barn with its brightly lit lanterns. And quite regularly now other men came straggling in, all looking suspiciously at Joe. They asked him many questions about Black Storm, and although Joe tried to put the matter away by telling them Black Storm was just an ordinary horse, he was aware that all of a sudden these men knew exactly that they were looking on the famous black horse that John Harney had made so much money with at Wichita.

The whole terrible danger he was in now came to Joe Bain in a flash. There was not a man in the place, so far as he could tell, that knew him. He was considered a horse thief!

The full danger of the situation was plain to
him for he knew in these turbulent times that
more than one innocent man in this situation
had lost his life, and only when it was too late
friends proved the victims innocent. In these
days these hard men who suspected anyone of
stealing a horse, killed the man first and made
inquiries afterward.

It was a most desperate situation and Joe
knew it. He knew that his only chance to get on
Black Storm and out of the livery stable alive
was to act as if he was not in the least suspicious
of what was in the men's minds. And he knew
men well enough, for in spite of his youth Joe
Bain was a born leader of men, one who understood their weaknesses as well as their
strength. He was armed and he was aware that
they knew he was a real man of the Old West,
with all that went with it. Seemingly doing it
without thinking he kept his eyes on them like
a hawk and before they were aware of it he had
led Black Storm about as if to see, as he said,
"if the stirrup would rub the wound"—until he
was in the doorway. As always, Joe's quirt was
swinging from its strap at his wrist. Although
smiling steadily in his seemingly natural way,
Joe's mind was on fire for he saw the men, all
in a half circle, standing nervously ready for
action and he knew that only his six shooter by
his side and his eyes on them now prevented

the first man of them from flashing his hand to his gun; yet Bain knew that was coming and it was coming mighty soon. If he got out alive he could not ride back on the trail. Men were always coming up on that trail at all hours of the night. Northeast there was no trail; he must ride northeast. There was no chance to get word to John Harney.

Joe knew that he still had time to beat them to the "draw," cover them, and still, it might be, escape in this way. But the danger in that would be that some man might come up from the outside with drawn revolver, then shooting and killing would have to be done.

Black Storm now stood in perfect position in the high doorway and Joe's hand rested lightly for the moment on the saddle horn. An inspiration came to him. "There's fire!" he shouted, pointing to the rear of the livery barn. What he said came so unexpectedly and so convincingly that every man whirled to look, since fires in these barns were not uncommon where there were many drinking men.

In that instant Joe Bain leaped in the saddle and struck Black Storm with the quirt. He leaped like a shot just as the men, seeing they had been deceived, whirled with drawn revolvers. They fired and yelled, but Black Storm was already out of sight. A man, hearing the firing and yelling of "Horse thief! Stop him!", drew his revolver and came running from the alley by the barn. Black Storm had no time to turn. He reared, struck the man terrifically, knocking him with a thud against the ground, leaped over him and rushed on.

Unfortunately, Joe did not dare run down the main street, the quickest way to his intended course, for now men were pouring out of the saloons and mounting their horses. The familiar, wild cries of "Horse thief! Stop him!" were on every man's tongue, and unless Joe had good luck, he might find men at any instant riding upon him from in front. He put Black Storm at a run down a side street, turned to the east, thinking fast as he did so. He had nearly cleared the town when he saw a half dozen mounted men riding down a street to intercept him. He turned Black Storm straight north and raced down another side street with its dimly lit frame buildings. Black Storm cleared the street and shot out on the open prairie. Like a swarm of rats fully fifty mounted men came in behind shooting and yelling.

Black Storm swept quickly out of range of the bullets and Joe had hope that he might ride it out with them straight north on the Pawnee cattle trail. This he certainly would have done had not some wily men anticipated him while he was dodging and turning, trying to get out of town. They had at once ridden out nearly two miles and thrown out their lines well on either side of the trail. In the moonlight Joe saw them and turned straight east, yet he knew he must not go too far in that direction for he would ride into almost certain death—another cow town, where there were many men like these pursuing him.

Across the open, rolling plains Black Storm rushed. Joe was fearful now that his horse might stumble, or worse still, step into a badger hole, but there was no other way.

He covered a mile with men coming on hard from the south and west, and as he passed down a dip in the prairie, he suddenly saw three riders coming toward him from the east! It happened that they were coming from another town but they heard the yells and understood. They began firing at Joe and a bullet whistled dangerously near him. Joe had lost valuable time in turning first north and then east and his skillful pursuers had taken advantage by cutting across in front.

And again those riding on the west, anticipating his move, whirled and lashed their horses hard toward the north. Joe was desperate now. All the men were armed with revolvers, and he must strive to keep out of range for he knew that, incensed as they were, they would strive to bring down Black Storm in order to get at their man.

North of him Joe knew the lay of the land. He knew where the river at one point cut in under a high precipitous clay bank, a mile long and fully thirty feet high. His mind worked frantically trying to discover some way of getting into the river and crossing under cover of the night. He was still out of range of those on his right, but to his astonishment he saw those ahead of him on the west beginning to come down at an angle to head him off. He was afraid that at any moment now some of them might fire a deadly shot at his beloved horse.

Then all of a sudden Joe made up his mind. The woods loomed a little beyond him, standing dark and silent on the long, high bank above the river.

Turning in his saddle, Joe poured a stream of fire towards those nearest and checked them. Then without a pause he rode at a run through the woods, the boughs of the trees knocking off his hat and almost blinding him. He brought Black Storm to the precipitous bank; he knew the river here. It was always deep, muddy, swift. Joe shouted at Black Storm to take the leap. Black Storm, as if he sensed the necessity, acted instantly. He leaped far out and down—it seemed he would never strike. Then horse and rider struck the deep water. Joe, for the moment, was half strangled. Black Storm quickly bobbed up, swimming. Swiftly, silently, he swam the narrow stream, and lunged out on the other side, and still on through the woods until he was out on the open sod. The river and a long fringe of willows and cottonwoods was now between him and his enemies.

"Our man's at bay in the woods," Joe heard the words from half a dozen excited men on the other side of the river.

Then a loud, deep, booming voice rolled out, "Surround that woods! Let every man stand ready! Keep back from his fire until daylight!"

This was music to the ears of Joe Bain. He was certain the men knew the country here, and evidently they had thought it impossible for him to make his horse leap from the precipice. He could hear the men on the other side of the river both below and above the woods at the point shouting to one another that they had taken their places.

Joe rode quietly along the other side for fully a mile letting Black Storm walk so that there would be very little sound from his hoofbeats. He then started forward at a canter and rode by easy stages until morning. With the coming of daylight, Joe was apprehensive again. He knew he might keep on this side of the river until noon, but by that time he must swim across or go very far out of his course.

A little before noon he reached a ford in the river, crossed over, and keeping a sharp lookout on all sides of him, rode on northward, but not on the beaten trail. He kept well east of it where he might, most of the time, ride in hiding behind low bluffs. Often he rode in deep depressions where he knew that Black Storm could not be seen by anyone passing along the main trail in either direction.

Black Storm was feeling fine and Joe had only to look at him—at his bright, alert eyes to know that Black Storm was as happy as a horse may be in his world. His wounded sides were both healing splendidly in the cool fall weather.

Joe began now feeling a growing sense of security as he rode along, and the thoughts that were uppermost in his mind were on Helen and the men at home. How surprised and glad they would all be at seeing Black Storm again safe and well, and as beautiful as he ever was; and how Helen would go on over him!

Joe was in such a mood that he began to look with pleasure at the landscape; for these wild plains, with their streams and belts of timber, were his life.

It was late in the afternoon and he was letting Black Storm walk as he approached a long line of timber growing on either side of a small creek. Joe had crossed many of these, and after looking closely ahead and seeing no signs of men, he let Black Storm have his head to pick his way through the woods, Joe sitting at ease in the saddle, both hands on the saddle horn.

It was an unusually wide stretch of woods, with here and there vast tangles of wild grape-vines hanging down from the tall trees like great ropes. Black Storm picked his way around several bramble tangles, pushed through the low thickets when there was no other way, until he was almost up to the creek.

Then all at once, as he stepped into a mass of tall, dead grass and bushes, a wild animal of some kind leaped out fairly under his feet. Fright struck him like lightning. He leaped so quickly and wholly unexpectedly that Joe Bain was almost unseated, and quicker than thought Black Storm shot under a long slim bough, then stopped, trembling like a leaf—stopped and turned back, for his rider was off his back, lying very still and pale on the leaves of the forest.

When Joe Bain opened his eyes he did not at first know what had happened and certainly did not know where he was nor how he came there. As his mind cleared he saw a grizzled old man bending over him—a man with long gray hair and beard, dressed in buckskin.

"Well, young feller," the old man was saying kindly, "you're coming out of it all right."

Joe turned his head a little. It was night, and he saw a small fire burning near.

"I was just coming down to the creek for water," the old plainsman explained, "when I saw you riding in the timber, and about the time I looked I saw your horse jump like a streak, and then I saw you strike that limb and go off."

"My horse," said Joe, "did he run off?"

"No, indeedy, he didn't run off!" the old man smiled. "A smart horse that. He turned right around the minute he found you were knocked off and when I came up he was standing with his nose close down to you like he was troubled about you. He moved back when I came up but when I carried you over here by the fire to keep you warm he walked right along behind me. I was afraid he would run off and tried to get hold of him to tie him but he wouldn't let me. He'd back away every time I tried it and after a while he went over and stood by my horse, tied to a tree there, as you see. But he would stand there only a little while when he would come over here and edge around, trying to get up to you but all the time seeming to be afraid I'd get hold of him. Finally I moved back to let him have his way and see what he would do. He came right up to you and put his nose on you and made little sounds acting for all the world like he was trying to wake you up, but when I came up he again backed away. He's standing over there now watching us."

Joe felt as if he was getting to himself and raised up on one elbow. "Come, Stormy," he said, and instantly Black Storm came up; he walked around the old plainsman and came to Joe on the other side.

Joe stroked him kindly, saying, "I'll be all right soon, Stormy. You did it but you didn't know."

The old man brought some water in his hat and bathed Joe's face and head.

"I've been doing this ever since I brought you up here," he said.

With the cold water on his face and head Joe felt better still. He sat up and said he was thirsty and hungry. The old plainsman gave him both meat and water. Joe wanted to mount and ride on, but at the old man's wish, gave in and slept until dawn.

When he mounted Black Storm, the old man said, "Don't ever blame your horse, young feller—he thinks a heap of you—I hope nothing bad happens to you or him."

"I think we'll make it home now," said Joe. And he told him who he was, adding, "I ought to reach home in a few days."

"If nothing else happens," added the old man seriously, "'pears like a man in these parts never knows when morning comes what's going to come before night—but good luck to you."

Joe thanked him kindly and with a wave of his hand rode out of the timber to the open plains. The old man looked after him saying,

"By cracky! A mighty fine young feller and a mighty fine horse! I hope nothing happens to them."

In the meantime Joe Bain was galloping rapidly out of sight, taking his chances by moving directly north on the Pawnee Trail. He was now heading straight toward the hills and valleys, the creeks and wild, deep gorges of the McDonald cattle range.

Once more Joe halted near a human being. This was at a stage coach inn where he bought some provisions for himself, and a small bag of oats. Then he mounted and again was away on the northern trail. Each night he halted a few hours to give the horse his rest, but always he halted in some lonely ravine with only the stars looking down upon them. On one of these nights Joe lay down on the withered buffalo grass and dozed. Black Storm had his complete freedom; he was neither tied nor hobbled for there was no need. After Joe had slept for a time, he was awakened by a soft velvet touch on his face and a low loving sound. Joe opened his eyes quickly and saw that Black Storm had come up to nose him—for Black Storm had at last become anxious when he saw Joe lying so long and so still on the earth. Joe put his hands upon the horse's head, got up and after patting him affectionately, mounted at once, and again they hurried away on the trail.

## Chapter XXI

### "THE PRAIRIE IS ON FIRE"

IT was late on that memorable afternoon when Joe Bain rode in on the east side of the McDonald range. Joe was glad he was so near home although he still had a number of miles to go. He could scarcely wait to get Black Storm to Helen and the others; and Black Storm was more eager than ever now.

Joe had entered the range on the east side where the country was broken with high hills and deep ravines. He rode over a ridge and down a bluff toward a winding, brush-covered gorge. Suddenly his horse shied and at the same time Joe heard the loud whinny of a horse in the ravine; he looked quickly and saw the sorrel horse of the under-foreman, Charlie Bliss, saddled and tied below to a tree. At the same time Charlie himself straightened up from behind some dense brush on the other side of the ravine.

"Joe!" the small, wiry under-foreman shouted, and then recognizing the horse he yelled, "How'd you ever get Black Storm?" Joe rode quickly up and the few words exchanged were quick and energetic.

"Thunder and lightnin'!" exclaimed Bliss, "just to think—I can't go in with you. I got to get a bunch of strays in."

Joe offered to help, but Bliss said, "No! No! You go on and let Helen see him." Then as Bain rode away Charlie yelled, "Joe, I forgot—Helen rode to the house north of the river to get some of her things. She left a note at the house—you better stop there first—she may be back. Mac and the boys have gone to town—won't be back till night—but likely Helen will be there by the time you are!"

"All right, Charlie!" Joe shouted, "I'll find her," and he galloped swiftly away.

Ill luck happened to Charlie Bliss on this evening. Elated at the coming of Black Storm he was in a great hurry. He wanted to drive the strays in quickly and get back at the ranch house. He ran to his horse; the nervous sorrel suddenly became frightened and leaped and lunged back so violently that before Charlie could get hold of him he broke his tether and was off like the wind toward the south. Charlie stopped, looked at the horse, and uttered the range language that only Charlie Bliss was capable of. He got up to the top of a ridge and to his unspeakable anger and disgust he saw the horse still running on to the south. Charlie breathed a heavy breath; he knew this meant a very long walk home. It was a distance great enough to try the heart of any cowboy for above all things, a cowboy hated to walk. But Charlie gathered up his rifle, which had fallen from its holster on the saddle when the horse reared, and started on the long walk home.

Joe Bain, of course, knew nothing of this; he was away and well out of sight when it happened. Joe reached the ranch house to find Helen's note on a small table. It read: "I've gone to the north ranch house to get some things. I'll be back by dark. Don't worry, Helen."

Joe laid the note on the table and going out to Black Storm said, "We'll surprise Helen, we'll go over toward the north ranch and meet her."

Black Storm was fresh and eager and when Joe mounted, he leaped along the trail pulling a little at the bit. The nearest route to the north

ranch lay across this valley, to the bridge on the
river near the Fort. Joe galloped down this trail
with the hoofbeats of Black Storm pounding
rapidly upon the hard ground. Just as they
reached the river bridge, there came to Joe the
unmistakable smell of prairie fire; he pulled up
his horse and looked. A thin veil of smoke
loomed in the sky almost straight north of the
Army Post. The Ogden Flats had a number of
times burned there with no great damage; Joe
supposed this was where the prairie was on fire.
A little fear went through him, but he at once
put it away. Of course, he thought, Helen could
see and of course she was already coming on
and Joe wanted to meet her very soon. He
crossed the bridge and rode up the gravelly
slope near one of the cavalry stables and was
about to put his horse to a gallop when he noticed with quick apprehension that his saddle
was slipping. Joe disliked to stop, but a loose
cinch might prove dangerous. He quickly dismounted and found the cinch partly broken;
with some strings of whang leather he finally
fixed it. This required a little time and he felt
a genuine uneasiness when he mounted and
again looked north. The line of fire there seemed to be extending toward the west.

"Come, Stormy!" Joe shouted, slapping Black
Storm lightly with the palm of his hand. With
a leap the horse started at a run down the road

leading west, passed through a thin line of woods to the clear when Joe saw something that made him forget Black Storm utterly.

The smell of fire was strong now and a little beyond him he saw some mounted cavalry galloping with an officer at their head. A line of fire was coming across the hill toward the Fort. The cavalrymen dismounted, and while some held the horses, others began beating the fire with wet gunny sacks.

Joe rode near the men. He recognized the officer, Captain Morse, and the officer at the same time recognized him. Morse rode up quickly saying, "This is a bad fire, Joe. I never saw a prairie fire come up so quickly. We'll have all we can do to keep it out of the Post!"

The fire was rushing down so near that both Black Storm and the horse of the officer became frightened.

Joe shouted, "Captain, I came out to meet Helen McDonald. She went to the north ranch house. Have you seen her?"

"No!" cried the officer.

"Then I'll ride to the ranch house and see," Joe shouted.

"Wait," the Captain shouted, "I'll send a man with you!"

But the only reply was Joe's words sounding faint and far in the drifting smoke. "Never mind, I'll make it alone!"

Joe shouted to Black Storm and the horse fairly flew in his race across the prairie. He shot out on the valley and thundered like a rushing train on toward the canyon trail.

Night fell dark with cloudy skies. Joe's mind was a storm of thoughts. He had seen no sign of fire in the exact direction of the ranch house—it was well to the west, and thus far it seemed to be sweeping on from the north and straight down on the Post. It had already burned itself out on the shale just north of the place where the troopers were fighting, and the long line of red tongues was licking up the grass toward the river.

As Black Storm ran across the valley Joe was puzzled. He wondered if Helen had reached the ranch house and left it. If so then he must meet her at any moment because the canyon trail was the only one that led from this place to the Fort road—and she had promised to be home by dark. It seemed she would not be caught in this—yet a score of things might have happened to her. Then Black Storm struck the canyon trail and started up toward the high table land above. Joe saw, when nearly at the top, a thing that shocked him—smoke looming in the skies far to the west. The fire swept by sharp, changing gusts of wind was already leaping and racing out in a long red line still north of the ranch house—but it was coming!

## Chapter XXII

## ALL FOR A MAN

*A*S Black Storm raced up to the top of the hill Joe saw another long line of troopers with wet gunny sacks fighting the fire. While some of the men beat the flames, others ran with sacks to a nearby spring at the head of the canyon, splashed the sacks in the water and ran back with them to the men who were beating the fire. So close did Bain pass them that he saw their sweating, blackened faces.

"Lord! What's up, I wonder?" exclaimed one of the troopers as the black horse shot past, his body low, racing like a streak through the night.

"Something bad, I reckon," shouted another man. "People likely be burned to death in this. Lord, ain't it awful!"

The fire was sweeping at an angle down across a trough in the hills as Black Storm reached the topmost ground of the highland. To the north Joe saw the demon raise its fiery tongues high on the upland, hissing and cracking, licking up the tall grass before it, and roar-

ing on in the night. Joe heard the green stems
of a shrub as it burned with a loud "ping."
High in the air the wind carried flaming bits of
rosin weeds; and grass stems hurled themselves
on to spread new flames ahead of the main fire.

Desperately Black Storm ran, already covered with sweat and groaning under the strain,
all because he knew it was the will of the man
on his back. Another mile—a quarter more, and
Joe saw the lone house standing, a dark shadow
on the prairie. Then a sick feeling went
through him—he saw the dim light of a lamp in
the window. And now Black Storm thundered
up, Joe leaped from the saddle and rushed in.
The small lighted lamp stood on a table; no one
was in that room. He burst into the other. He
was dumbfounded to see Helen lying peacefully
asleep on her old bunk in the room. Joe ran to
her, jerked her up. She screamed in fright, then
saw who it was.

"Helen, the prairie's on fire!" Joe shouted.
He seized a man's old yellow raincoat that lay
across a chair, threw the coat around her and
shouted, "Where's your horse?"

"Oh, Joe," she cried, "he broke his leg in a
badger hole—I fell and hurt my ankle, that's
why I stayed—I can't walk!"

While she was speaking Joe seized her in his
arms and rushed out to Black Storm, leaped into the saddle, and swung Helen up behind him.

Black Storm needed no word for he knew fully the danger. He whirled and shot like a rocket toward the south while Helen's arms gripped Joe like a vise.

"The river," Joe shouted, "we must get to the river!"

There were now at times sharp gusts of wind that blew the fire in every direction, and flying embers of dead grass were constantly being blown far ahead of the blaze, and at once seething flames shot up from that point while the wall of flame came roaring on behind.

It was a fearful ride, together as they were, on the leaping, rushing Black Storm, and only skilled riders could have hoped to stay on. On they rushed, trying to make the canyon trail on the south. As Black Storm swept up on a little rise of ground they saw a long line of flames rushing at an angle toward them, and then to their astonishment saw the flames racing across the valley from the west! The treacherous wind with flying embers had struck there also; a groan came from Joe Bain. But one chance was left. There was still a streak on the east where the gray prairie stood untouched. It came over Joe in a flash—if he could get through this streak before it caught fire, he could reach the burned-over ground where he had seen the troopers fighting just east of the trail. Helen cried and clung to him when she saw Black

Storm himself was turning to the left. "We must try this way," Joe shouted.

Black Storm was now rushing through blue-stem grass that was so tall it brushed Joe's feet in the stirrups. He felt it and urged Black Storm the harder. And while Helen gripped tight, Joe's lips moved in something like whispered prayer—she *must* not die in this! Strange thoughts swept through his brain. He remembered the troopers who had been fighting here. They probably were now moving back across the belt of woods near the Post. Perhaps they were laughing and joking about their faces; pretty soon they would all be washed up and sleeping peacefully in their bunks. And here he was with Helen. Ah! how terribly unjust that Helen should be here—and Black Storm, the beloved horse—yet only Black Storm might save them and he was still rushing hard—ah! how terribly he was running, his nostrils wide, his black coat covered with foam, his powerful muscles knotted and his breath coming in great heaving groans.

On the north the whole heavens were lit up in a lurid glare, and that awful steady roaring and crackling sounded louder in the sheets of flame. As Black Storm plunged forward jack-rabbits ran before him. A wave of dense smoke drove down to bewilder temporarily Joe and Helen, but the horse rushed on the harder—

driving toward the opening. Ah! Joe thought,
if they could only have been at this point
quicker. A wave of heat swept across their faces.
Black Storm shot across a little barren ridge, his
hoofs kicking up gravel and small stones to send
them flying in the rear. A coyote ran alongside
for a moment but Black Storm did not shy—
only rushed on with greater speed. The line of
flames on the east was about to cut them off.
Black Storm himself saw and wheeled a little
south. All that Joe knew now was that he was
running the horse toward a long water-filled
gulch to the southeast. If he could make this
gulch with its water and red clay banks—they
would try that!

The gulch—that was it! It could not be far
beyond now, only a little more to the south!
He remembered seeing the sweating, blackened
troopers standing on the burned prairie fighting the flames just east of that place. Yes, they
must be near the gulch. Another blinding wave
of smoke; Black Storm still plunged on but the
raging fire now cut them off and he whirled,
leaped like a hound, knowing what he did, but
there was no other way. And then—the earth
seemed to give way. What was this? Was it a
terrible delirium? But no—in a flash Joe understood it all. He knew he was still on the horse,
Helen still holding to him in the strangling
smoke. Black Storm had leaped over a danger-

ous steep shale slope of the ravine because it had been that or death to all. With a groan he went down on his haunches, plowing through the shale of the steep at a fearful rate. Joe felt a choking sensation. How many times he had ridden past this long, dangerous shale slope when he was hunting stray Longhorns! And how many times he had said to himself it would be mighty bad if a man rode along there on a dark night and his horse shied off. It was more than a hundred feet down the slope to the small stream below. Near the bottom there was an overhanging rocky ledge; over this Black Storm fell and both Joe and Helen were hurled over his head to fall hard on the gravel below.

Black Storm fell hard, so hard he broke the cinch of the saddle and it slipped from him. For a moment he felt sick and weak but was soon himself again and got to his feet among some round, gray rocks where he had fallen. Both his knees were skinned and bleeding, and blood was trickling down his head where he had struck glancingly on a rock. Breathing hard and quivering in every fiber he at once turned to look for his friends. He came up to them to find them lying still on the shale completely dazed, Joe still talking and thinking they were running from the fire.

Black Storm walked up and put his nose down on Joe, rubbed him and uttered low sounds, then he pushed Joe a little harder and tried in vain to get him to be as he had always been, but his master paid no heed to him. Then Black Storm timidly put his nose on Helen. He made sounds to her also but she would not move or talk to him, except to groan; and again he came back to Joe and began to nose him.

This seemed to start Joe's brain working for he staggered to his feet, still not knowing what he was doing for he believed he was still on Black Storm running from the fire. And now a strange thing happened. Although Joe had never used the quirt on Black Storm he always carried the whip, as a matter of custom, letting it hang from his wrist. He now lashed out wildly with the whip, striking Black Storm a stinging blow, the while crying incoherently.

Amazed, his heart cut to the quick because he could not understand, Black Storm did not leap back as he would if he had been struck by another man. He only flinched at the pain, then turned and walked away.

At this moment there came a flash of lightning followed by a crash of thunder. Black Storm threw up his head. A great black cloud had been fast coming up as so often happened after these prairie fires, and in a moment the cold rain drove down in torrents.

For a little Black Storm stood looking back at him who lay again, so still on the little level before the rock—stood, looking, unmindful of the cold and the rain, unmindful of the cracking of the thunder. The hot sweat and foam was still streaming from him when the rain struck, and now, although he was being suddenly cooled, he was so tired—and so disappointed. He walked across the little stream and started away on the valley, halted once and looked back longingly, started on and again stopped, and again started on. His master had struck him a stinging blow. For some reason then, his master did not want him now, so he would travel home. He could not understand it at all. If he could not remain with the one man in the world he would then go home where the master lived—the master's home—that was calling him now—that, it seemed, would be as near to him as he could get at this time. The saddle was gone and the reins of the bridle were still over his head so that they did not impede him.

On the same trail over which he had before rushed so hard with a storm in his soul, he now made his way back only to move in another kind of storm; and his life, for the most part, had meant to him only storm—storm and battle, disappointment, misery and in it all complete mystery. He had been very weary when the storm struck, but now the cold rain refreshed him. It seemed to him he should get home more quickly and he broke into a trot.

## Chapter XXIII

### A MAN AND HIS HORSE

*T*HROUGH wind and driving rain that night. John McDonald and a number of his men were galloping across the east valley toward home. Late that evening McDonald had seen in the distance the prairie fire in the north and he said to himself that he was glad he had moved to this side of the river. He and the men, seeing the threatening sky, had left the town and started for home, but they had not covered more than half the distance when the driving sheets of rain struck them. They were wet to the skin, and the cold rain chilled McDonald and the men through and through. They supposed, however, they would soon be in the comfort of a warm lighted home, and John never doubted that Helen would be there awaiting him.

As McDonald, therefore, riding a little ahead of the men, came up to the house, he saw with great surprise there was no light there. Something was wrong. He swung from the saddle at the door and let his horse trot on to the stable with the men. Inside the house he called the name of Helen. But there was no answer, only the driving wind and rain against the ranch house. McDonald fumbled in the darkness, found the matches and lighted an oil lamp on the table. Instantly he saw Helen's note. With the water streaming from his clothing to the floor he picked up the note and read it. An exclamation of astonishment escaped him. He ran quickly to the other rooms. They were empty. At the same time there sounded outside the voice of a man complaining.

John McDonald started toward the door, but before he could reach it, it swung open and Charlie Bliss fairly staggered in. Charlie had seen what he knew to be a bad prairie fire in the north as he came over the hills toward home, but supposed he would find both Helen and Joe safely at the house. When he burst in and found Helen not yet arrived he quickly told McDonald of Joe getting Black Storm and of his words when he rode away. The men, dripping wet, came pouring in to stand and to listen in amazement at the words of Charlie Bliss. The same thought went through the mind of every man. Helen and Joe would have been home long before this unless something bad had happened. Helen had gone to the house far north of the river—that was what made them fearful.

At this moment came the wild, shrill neigh of a horse outside, rising high, piercing above the roar of the storm. They opened the door but at first could see nothing. Both Charlie Bliss and John McDonald hurried out; then, when the lightning glared, Charlie shouted, "Mac! It's Black Storm, his bridle's on him, but the saddle's gone!"

"Get the men to the horses!" shouted McDonald, as he ran toward the stable. "We'll ride north of the river!"

Out in the night, through the driving rain the men ran to the stables. In the excitement they forgot Black Storm, but when they had mounted and started away at a run they were aware, when there came a bright flash of lightning, that he was galloping with them.

It flashed in the mind of Charlie Bliss that the horse would be lost again, but there had been no time to do anything now. Then John McDonald saw in another blinding flash that Black Storm was running ahead of them on the trail that led to the river bridge. Then Charlie Bliss, who was riding hard in front also saw Black Storm running on ahead. The other men were rushing on close behind.

"Charlie!" McDonald shouted in Bliss' ear, "I wonder if that horse knows what he's doing or does he just want to be with the other horses!"

"We'll watch him if he turns!" shouted Charlie, "but likely he's just scared and running because he's with the rest of us!"

The cold rain drove in the men's faces, down their necks, and in spite of coats they were drenched to the skin. It was not merely a rain —the water drove down in a flood from the skies. The horses, splashing almost constantly through running water, shook their heads in protest and tried to turn, but loud yells from their riders drove the animals forward. They rushed across the bridge, Black Storm's hoofs thundering on ahead of them. Two miles up the valley toward the west and they swept on past the target grounds when suddenly Black

Storm turned to the right. There was no guess-work now. He knew what he was doing, and there was never a question about it. Straight to a little ravine he ran. The small stream here was now rushing along four feet deep. Black Storm did not hesitate, and the men saw, in a glare, the black form of the horse as he plunged across. McDonald drove his horse in the stream and Charlie Bliss splashed in behind him. Again they saw Black Storm; he plunged up the shale slope to a little level and stopped. The men came up, swung from their horses and stood near the jutting rock.

Joe Bain, pale as ashes, was on his feet with his hands on Black Storm, and Helen, too, was on her feet.

"Thank God," exclaimed John McDonald, as he put his arms around Helen. "Are either of you hurt?" he shouted.

"No," exclaimed Joe and Helen in a breath. "But Black Storm, Father," cried Helen, "he saved us from the fire in an awful race, but fell with us here—when Joe and I came to our senses he was gone—Joe thinks, in his bewilder-ment, he struck him—how did he—"

The storm was beating so fiercely that Helen cut off her words, and she and Joe both mounted Black Storm, and they all started back on the trail, the horses splashing in water con-stantly, the lightning filling the whole valley with blinding flashes, and peal after peal of thunder crashing from the heavens to shake the earth under their feet.

As they battled on through the storm John McDonald shouted out in jerky sentences to Helen all that they knew of Black Storm's presence.

Black Storm was galloping in the center of the horses and he seemed to be able to keep the pace although time after time, in spite of the storm, Joe Bain called out to them to hold back a little, for Black Storm was in no shape to be pushed hard even in all this.

At last they passed over the long north trail, recrossed the river bridge and came out on the wide valley on the south; the rain was now slackening rapidly. When they finally reached the ranch house the storm had ceased altogether and there came a strange stillness with dark, restless clouds rolling across the sky.

The horses were put away and Black Storm was led into a quiet, clean stall.

Cold and wet, all went in to put on dry clothing, all except Joe Bain, who stayed with his horse.

They came out in a little time with all four lanterns from the house for they must see Black Storm well.

They found Joe working over him and trying to rub him dry, when Helen said, "Joe, you are wet and cold, you must go in and get some dry clothing."

"I guess I forgot about that," he said. "I'll be out again in a minute."

When Joe left him, Black Storm began to be very restless, constantly turning his head and uttering anxious sounds. They talked to him and patted him, but could not quiet him.

Joe Bain was gone but a very few minutes. He knew that Black Storm was ill from the terrible strain, but as yet he had said nothing to the others. Joe came out and entered the stall. Black Storm put his head up to him and groaned, then his head dropped low. He felt so sick now and his suffering was extreme. Joe took the halter from his head and said, "Lie down, Stormy, hadn't you better lie down?"

Slowly Black Storm dropped to his knees, then lay down at full length in the stall. His eyes could be seen in the light of the lanterns—eyes that cannot be described, but they told all who looked that he was so sick.

John McDonald's voice was a little unsteady when he said, "Joe, we're going to town to telegraph to Kansas City for a veterinary. If money can save this horse, he'll be saved."

In less than five minutes McDonald and two of his men were riding hard across the wet, moonlit valley toward the town. Steadily, rapidly, they galloped until they pulled up their horses at the little dimly lit depot. There would not be a train until eleven o'clock in the morning, the agent said.

John McDonald stood with a depressed look on his face. "I had hoped we might get the doctor earlier," he said, "but we'll have to do the best we can."

The message was sent and again he and his men rode back, and again they hurried, yet fearing for the worst.

All that night Black Storm lay suffering in the stall, and all night Helen and the men worked over him, trying to sweat him with heavy covering and doing all they knew.

When morning dawned and the sun came up to shine peacefully on the world there was no change in Black Storm. He was so sick that he would not even look at water. The hours of the forenoon dragged terribly. Helen walked to the brow of the hill time after time, looking across the valley toward the town, wringing her hands and saying, "Oh, won't that train ever come!"

Joe came out to look also, but he would only look at his watch and go back to Black Storm. There was a deep, haggard look in Joe's face. He had touched no food since the trouble.

Finally, as Helen once more stood on the hill with something like a whispered prayer on her lips, she saw a distant speck far down the valley and then she heard the faint, faraway whistle of the train. She raced like a deer to the barn to tell them.

"Now, Joe," she said, "the doctor will soon be here. Father will be waiting with two horses at the buckboard and he's promised he'll put the horses at a run all the way here."

Slowly, it seemed, like the creep of a snail, the train came on to the station at Fort Riley, stopped there, it seemed for ages, before it started, then on it came for the three short miles to Junction City.

Helen did not leave the hill, but stood and watched. Presently she saw coming across the valley the buckboard with the horses at a fast gallop. The doctor was coming. On they came, nearer and nearer and nearer and at last were at the stable. The doctor with his medicine case came at once into the stall and began examining Black Storm.

"A beautiful horse—too bad," were his first words.

After a long examination, he said, "The chances for him are about even. About three days will tell the story. I'll see that all's done that can be done." And taking off his coat the doctor called for some water and began to mix some medicine. All that afternoon at regular intervals, he had Joe give Black Storm the

medicine through a long necked bottle. Black
Storm did not protest when Joe gave it to him
although he did spill some of the medicine because he did not know what to do.

All that night the doctor remained up with
him and until noon the next day. Then to the
delight of all Black Storm raised his head, drew
a long, deep, natural breath and whinnied
when Joe rubbed his nose. A bucket of water
was brought. Black Storm drank it and licked
the bottom of the bucket for more. They gave
him another bucket full and he drank it eagerly, then got to his feet and sniffed to his feed
box.

The doctor smiled. "He's out-guessed me," he said, "I thought if he made it at all it would take three days and he's made it in a night and half a day. A remarkable horse. He's got lots of heart. He'll soon be well now. I'm glad to have served him and the rest of you."

The doctor left on the evening train. After night had fallen on the McDonald home, they lit the lanterns and again all went to see Black Storm. Joe Bain had lain down for a little sleep, but he heard them going out and he got up and also went out. And then as Joe Bain came out of the house he made a sound in his throat and Black Storm heard. He looked toward the door, his eyes wide, uttering a constant succession of whinnying sounds. Then as Joe came in he put his hands on Black Storm's head, a head that nestled very close to him and Black Storm closed his eyes, drew a long breath, and stood hushed and still like a weary child.

In the shadow of the stall on the other side of him stood Helen McDonald with one arm over him. For a moment her lips rested against his neck, and in the silence the tears ran down her cheeks to fall upon him.

"Dear Stormy," she whispered with quivering lips, in tones so low they were meant only for him, "I love you and so do we all."

The men stood silent, the night outside was hushed and the little stall was very still.

For a list of other books by Thomas C. Hinkle,
see the following pages.

# BOOKS BY THOMAS C. HINKLE

WOLF: A Range Dog
BLACKJACK: A Ranch Dog
JUBE: The Story of a Trapper's Dog
SHEP: A Collie of the Old West
OLD NICK AND BOB: Two Dogs of the West
DUSTY: The Story of a Wild Dog
BARRY: The Story of a Wolf Dog
CRAZY DOG CURLY
KING: The Story of a Sheep Dog
BING: The Story of a Tramp Dog
SHAG: The Story of a Dog
BUGLE: A Dog of the Rockies
TAWNY: A Dog of the Old West